D1287897

BEYOND PARADISE

BEYOND PARADISE

Jane Hertenstein

Morrow Junior Books New York

Published by Morrow Junior Books
a division of William Morrow and Company, Inc.
1350 Avenue of the Americas, New York, NY 10019
www.williammorrow.com

Printed in the United States of America.

10 9 8 7 6 5 4 3 2 1

Library of Congress Cataloging-in-Publication Data
Hertenstein, Jane.
Beyond paradise / Jane Hertenstein.
p. cm.
Summary: Within months of arriving in the exotic Philippines from Upper Sandusky, Ohio, to live with her missionary parents on the island of Panay, fourteen-year-old Louise finds herself a prisoner of war in an internment camp when the Japanese invade her new country in 1941.
ISBN 0-688-16381-5
1. Philippines—History—Japanese occupation, 1942–1945—Juvenile fiction. 2. World War, 1939–1945—Philippines—Juvenile fiction. [1. Philippines—History—Japanese occupation, 1942–1945—Fiction. 2. World War, 1939–1945—Philippines—Fiction. 3. Prisoners of war—Fiction.] I. Title.
PZ7.H432435Bg 1999 [Fic]—dc21 99-19037 CIP

To Mom—you see, I told you I would.

BEYOND PARADISE

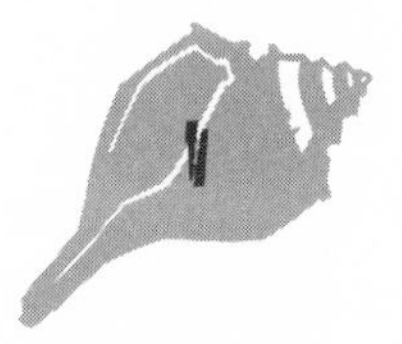

Beyond Cleveland, Beyond Columbus

Boom!

The sudden sound penetrated my deep, silent sleep. As if by reflex, my body shook and then relaxed into the pillows and clean white bedsheets.

"Daisy," said a woman's voice nearby, "please close the door quietly."

"Okay, Mama. Did she wake up yet?"

"Do you mean Louise, honey? Yes, she's awake, but she's still a little groggy from her sickness."

The muffled echo of bare feet pulled me further from my stupor. I opened my eyes to peer through a veil of mosquito netting; everything seemed pale and dreamlike. "Where am I?" I asked.

A woman's kind face bent over me and folded back the netting. "You're at the Baptist missionary compound. You arrived here a few days ago with your parents, but you were so sick with fever that you had to be carried from the ferry. You must be feeling better now, I see."

I nodded, remembering vaguely the ferryboat trip from Manila to the outer islands of the Philippines. My head had pounded as the weighted motors down below in the ferry snorted like an old man sleeping, blowing air out through his green rudder teeth. Salty seawater misted and sprayed the deck. I clung to the railing, looking out over the Visayan Sea, which was dotted with islands too numerous for names. My brain seemed to be made of cobwebs as I tried to remember what had happened.

I had come out from Ohio with my mother and father to the Philippines. Papa had taken a position to head up a missionary school on the island of Panay. I looked around the sunny bedroom where I now lay. Someone was missing. "Julie?" I called out.

"No, my name is Ann. Ann Fletcher—your new neighbor at the compound." Ann spoke with a strong Southern accent. "Your mother is downstairs resting, and your father went with Frank, my husband, to the dock to retrieve your trunks."

I tried to lift myself out of the bed, but collapsed backward onto the pillows. The fever had left my body achy and my muscles sore. Nausea swept over me as if I were still on the ferry, rolling. I remembered the trip out to Manila on the steamship from San Francisco. At the docks in San Francisco I had waved good-bye to my sister, Julie. She was staying back for one more year to finish high school before joining us in the Philippines. The fog had been thick that October day as we pulled out of the bay. Straining my eyes, I looked into the crowd for one last glimpse of her face.

We had docked for a day in Hawaii, where I met some native fishermen beside a strange boat—a slim, narrow sailboat with a bar on the side to balance it. They had talked and laughed, and when they saw me, a man with almost-black skin reached inside the outrigger and pulled out a conch shell. Its pink pearly petals opened up to me

like a flower. He motioned to me to hold it up to my ear, laughing at my surprise. I could hear the sea, swishing and roaring inside the shell.

Once again a wave of nausea came over me. I shook my head to erase the sounds, forcing myself to sit up in the bed.

"I must have fallen ill on the ferryboat trip from Manila," I said. "I remember watching at the railing as the water turned from a pretty crystal blue to a seasick green. Is it malaria? I read about malaria before coming out. More Yanks were killed from malaria during the Spanish-American War than from the actual fighting."

Ann fluffed up the pillows stacked behind my head. "No, I don't think it is malaria, just a bad stomach flu that put you out for a few days. You'll be up in no time."

Boom! The door banged shut a second time. A very small girl rushed into the room. Her curly hair made her look identical to the other little girl staring up at me beside my bed. With big-sister attention the older child said, "Looky, the girl woke up."

"Yes, sweet peas. Louise did wake up, but she needs her rest."

The bigger child approached my bedside. "I'm Daisy. I'm five years old, and this is my little sister, Mae. She's two and a half. Mama says we are her sweet peas, and Mrs. Urs calls us little schnitzels. What's a schnitzel?"

I laughed. "I'm not sure, though I think you girls are very, very cute. I know we will be the greatest of friends."

"Now shoo, little peas." Ann turned to me and took my hand. "I'm sure we'll also be the best of friends. I'll check in on you in a bit."

All three left the room with yet another bang. I was

now fully awake and alert to the fact that I was in a new place. Nothing about this room reminded me of home. Sunshine flooded in through the open window shades. In the air was the smell of salt water and citrus fruits. The faint rustling of wings caught my attention. Tucked into a sunny corner of the bedroom was an orange-and-bright-green parakeet perched within a golden cage.

"Now," I said to myself, "I know I'm not in Upper Sandusky, Ohio. Have I died and gone to heaven?"

I crawled out of bed and lifted the little bar on the cage. The bird jumped to my outstretched finger and tilted his head to the side. Immediately he let out a twitter. I sat back on my heels in the bed, amazed at how far I had come.

"How would you like to go to paradise?" Papa asked with a twinkle in his eye. Paradise. It all began last spring when Judson Smith, a missionary home on furlough, came to see Papa at the church. Papa pastored the First Baptist Church of Upper Sandusky, Ohio. A dull gray church with solemn rules against card playing and dancing and, in general, having fun.

Judson Smith shared the pulpit with Papa Easter Sunday, April 1941. I remembered the day as being oppressively beautiful. It seemed a sin to be stuck inside a church building in springtime, singing the words to an old hymn: "This is my Father's world, / The birds their carols raise, / The morning light, the lily white, / Declare their Maker's praise." I strained my eyes to look through the brightly sunlit stained-glass windows.

"Thank you, Reverend Keller, for allowing me to join

you this day. I always enjoy visiting old friends." With his thin hair combed from the back of his head toward the front to cover a huge bald spot, Judson Smith looked older than Papa. Mr. Smith and Papa had gone to seminary together years ago.

"'Go ye into all the world, and preach the gospel.'" said Rev. Smith. "Yea, even unto the ends of the earth. To mountaintops, to the valleys below, yes, even to the wildest jungles. Friends, let us not be fainthearted and shrink back, but let us persevere and endure. I exhort you to support our missionaries in the city of Iloilo on the island of Panay in the Philippines."

A cloud passed in front of the stained glass. The pane depicting the Crucifixion darkened, and Mary's face took on a deeper shade of concern. I looked over at Mother. She stared straight ahead, her back rigid against the pew. Mother's face was beautiful, but in a fragile sort of way. Her lips spread thin, motionless in the shifting light. Julie, my older sister by three years, sat on the other side of Mother. Julie reminded me of the cartoon illustration of Snow White with her black hair shaped around a perfectly sweet face. Her red lips were tied into a bow, smiling, laughing, singing. Baptists were not allowed to go to the movie house; nevertheless, I often heard Julie humming "Someday My Prince Will Come."

"Go ye into all the world, and preach the gospel." I could not imagine Julie or Mother going to the ends of the earth; I could not even imagine them leaving Upper Sandusky. I, on the other hand, had flowing through my veins an urgency to run away, to fall off the face of the earth. But in all my fourteen years I had never been anywhere. I dreamed of dreaming in other languages, of waking up in other sunlight, of being someone else other than who I was, Jean Louise Keller.

After church that afternoon, around the dinner table, Rev. Smith bored us with stories about the Philippines. Of course, Julie and I were not allowed to leave the table while our guest lounged. We were obligated to sit and listen to him prattle on and on.

My bones ached and my mind wandered until I heard him talk about the Moro headhunters and how they cannibalized their victims. "Have you ever seen them?" I asked, interrupting his story.

"Well, I have met a few Moros in my day walking the trails, but they were civilized ones. Not the heathens who occupy the mountainous jungles. No," he said, "it takes much perseverance to teach these poor primitive people the ways of the gospel. . . ." On and on he talked. I envisioned Rev. Judson Smith's bald head sticking out of the top of a big, boiling pot, the long strand of hair covering his bald patch floating in the cauldron, his mouth opening and closing, talking endlessly about the stupidity of the "primitive people."

I laughed out loud. Everyone turned to look at me. Embarrassed, I said, "Continue, Reverend Smith. Tell us more."

"Arlen, you and Kate should consider the mission field. There is a *great* need for men of your caliber over there. The Baptist Church is looking for qualified pastors such as yourself to help teach in the less remote areas. Some of the islands have no Protestant clergy. The Catholics have their own services, but, of course, not everyone is a Catholic. Have you ever given thought to foreign service?"

A worried look crossed Mother's face. Mother could never be separated from Father. Mother had met Papa, fresh out of seminary, at a church ice-cream social. Papa said it was love at first sight, which always made Mother blush; her eyes, bright like points of light, never left Papa's face as she absorbed his every word.

Papa chuckled. "No, I don't think that life is for me. I like adventure, but would never consider leaving my family behind for the Philippines." He held mother's hand.

"Bring them with you, of course. Many families go over. There are ten of us in the compound in Iloilo City. We are considering starting up a Christian school for the native children. A wonderful opportunity for someone of your academic nature."

And that's how it all started. A couple of months later, Papa asked me, "How would you like to go to paradise?"

After the news of our intended departure was announced, I became a real heroine at school. Sarah Jane Addams, the most popular girl, who had snubbed me all my grade-school life, suddenly wanted to be pen pals with me. I think she merely wanted to add Philippine stamps to her collection.

I tried to explain Panay to Tyler, a neighborhood boy about one year younger than me, and much more gullible. Tyler's hair was so white and thin that I could see the blue veins in his skull pop out. We used to take long walks by the railroad tracks, watching the double-decker trains roll by. Men and women, mannequin-like, stared out the window at us and our little town. They were traveling, perhaps, to Cleveland or Columbus.

"We are moving away beyond Cleveland, beyond

Columbus," I said, "across the ocean to live on an island in the Pacific. I guess I got my wish to leave Upper."

"My auntie left Upper," said Tyler. "She moved to New York City and works in a skyscraper downtown. She says that if you drop a penny off the Empire State Building it will crush a car."

I ignored him. "It's hard to believe I'll be leaving in a little over a month. I've always wanted to run ten thousand miles and go in a hundred different directions. It's been my dream to travel, and now"—I scuffed the ground beside the railroad tracks with my foot—"it seems scary to go so far away."

Tyler wasn't paying any attention. "So I asked her, What if you dropped a nickel—"

I gave Tyler a knock on his transparent head. "At first I was mad that Julie got to stay. It's unfair that grown-ups always expect us kids to act responsible, and then when I volunteered to stay back with Julie, Mother said I was too young." I sighed, wondering about adult illogic. "But now I'm excited to be going, to get out of here. I can't stand the other kids at school. Why, the other day Sarah Jane Addams made a joke about my pop being a pastor. She asked if I wore holy underwear."

Tyler cast a sidelong glance at my backside. Again I had to give him a shove to keep him on track. "Of course, I'll miss Julie, but after she graduates next year she'll come out and meet us in the Philippines. Hey, Tyler, do you realize that it is already tomorrow across the international date line?"

"If it's tomorrow there, then what is today—yesterday?"

"They're twelve hours ahead of us. If we're going to

bed in Ohio, they're just waking up in Panay to a new day."

"Then do they know who won the Indians–White Sox game?"

I shook my head in disbelief and jumped down off the railroad tracks. Starting off across the baseball diamond behind the high school, I turned around and yelled at Tyler, "When I'm in the jungles of Panay, I'm going to run around buck naked just like the ladies in *National Geographic.*" Even at a distance I saw his blue veins bulging.

I rose up out of the bed to return the bird to his perch. Looking out the window and across the lawn, I saw groves of fruit trees fade into forests of palms and oversize frond trees. I was reminded of the verse from Revelation that Papa had read to Mother and me on our last night aboard the steamship; the Bible had spoken of destruction and ruin, and then of a new city. I whispered aloud, "'A new heaven and a new earth.'"

2

A New Heaven, a New Earth

AT THE MISSION COMPOUND I was soon up and around. It took awhile to adjust to the intense heat and humidity. It was November, and my short-sleeved cotton dress felt hot and suffocating. My head was still swimming from all the new faces and names. There were thirteen of us missionaries at the compound, along with a small group of Filipinos hired to do the chores. A regular bowl of mixed nuts. The Fletchers and their two girls hailed from Mississippi; the Albrights, another couple, also came from the United States; and a Swiss family, Flora and Johannes Urs, lived on the other side of our cottage. Alice Gundry had her own place. She had come out from Australia about twenty years ago and stayed. Pastor Judson Smith sort of ran the mission. I was the only teenager at the compound except for the Urses' fifteen-year-old son, Freddy, who was away at boarding school in Manila and due to come home during the December holiday break.

Papa was scheduled to go to Manila in about a week to pick up Freddy and the missionary schoolteacher. Her boat was expected December sixth. All three, plus numerous supplies, would return via interisland ferry.

After getting moved into our own cottage, Mother and I were invited to a luncheon—a welcoming party at Mrs. Albright's cottage. Ann Fletcher, Mrs. Albright, Mrs. Urs, and Alice Gundry were all waiting in a small sitting room to greet Mother and me.

Before going in, I saw a flash of hesitancy cross Mother's face. Being around so many new faces, new acquaintances, especially without Papa, made Mother shy. She seemed so frail, pale, and all alone. I couldn't imagine why she had agreed to come to the Philippines. On her own she would still be at home making a pudding for supper, lining up the wet laundry on the clothesline, stopping for a moment to straighten the tablecloth in the dining room. She had come because of Papa. I squeezed Mother's hand to let her know I was nearby. She hardly seemed to recognize my effort.

After the initial greetings and introductions, the conversation shifted to the new school Papa was to administrate. "We are all very keen about getting the school up and running," said Ann Fletcher. "It will be good to know that our own children will be receiving a Christian education without having to send them off to boarding schools."

"Yah, I want my Freddie closer to home," Mrs. Urs said. "Too many bad things happening everywhere. Hitler is taking over the world."

I had been hearing a lot about Hitler on the radio. Adolf Hitler was like a hungry locust chewing on a leaf. He had gobbled up Czechoslovakia, Poland, Belgium, Holland, Denmark, Norway, and France. On and on the hungry locust ate.

Back in Ohio, Papa had said that what happened in Europe didn't have anything to do with the United States.

Many of the people living in Upper were of German descent. Mr. Staub ran the drugstore and soda fountain. All the negative talk about Germans worried him.

I had asked Papa about the war and Hitler. "Are we going to have to go over and fight the Germans, Papa?"

"People are saying a lot of ugly things right now. Many people want to fight. I'm not saying Hitler is right; I don't believe we should go over there and solve Europe's problems."

"Winston Churchill wants the United States to come fight. If we do fight, what will happen to Mr. Staub? Will he have to go back to Germany?"

Papa had answered, "Who is American? Staub, Gottlieb, McSweeney, Keller, and Sullivan. It's like saying green, blue, and black belong to us, and you are red and yellow and brown. No. We are all together and all mixed up."

I thought about this now as the women's conversation continued. I felt safe tucked away in the Philippines, in paradise. Here in the Pacific, Europe was even farther away from us than it had been when we lived in Ohio.

"I don't like how the Japs are stirring things up in Chiner," Alice Gundry said. I had noticed right away that she spoke her mind.

We removed to the dining room, where three Filipino houseboys wearing white gloves and white uniforms served us a delicious dinner of rice, meat covered in curry sauce, grated coconut, and fried shrimp. On a lazy Susan sat smaller dishes of salted nuts, cheeses, and mango chutney sauce. There was also a salad of pears, dates, and figs—all imported onto the island. Later, under the whirling fans, we ate white cake and vanilla ice cream.

My stomach felt swollen and shaky. I wasn't accustomed to such rich food, especially after just getting over the stomach flu. I asked to be excused and started back to our cottage. Outside, on the gravel path, I met Arturo, the Filipino gardener, who was raking the lawn. His old body shaped itself around the handle of the rake. "Hello, miss." With only two teeth in his entire mouth, he looked up at me, smiling. I awkwardly smiled back.

"Hello. You speak very good English, Arturo."

"Yes, miss. Speak very good English. As a boy I grow up in Intramuros—the oldest part of Manila. My family had a house in the plaza." Arturo rested on his rake, his eyes distant, remembering his English, remembering an old story.

"Some of the nuns I didn't like. I, of course, learn Spanish, but one sister, she teaches me the catechism in English. When the American soldiers come, there is fighting in the countryside. The soldiers stay at the convent, and part of it is used for a hospital. I run errands for the nurses. One soldier knew I spoke English. He gave to me a book."

"What was that book?" I asked, attempting to take his rake.

"No, no. I do," he said, pushing me aside.

"Arturo, let me do it. Let me help."

He looked at me, perplexed.

"What was the book the soldier gave you to read?"

"*Huckleberry Finn.* A boy and a black man sail together on a wide river. I liked the story. That soldier good to me. I found him the best fruit in the market and shined his boots. When he left to go back to the States, he send to me a postcard."

"I've brought over a few books. You may borrow them if you like. Mostly poetry books. Do you like poetry, Arturo?"

"Oh, yes, I have read the poetry of José Rizal. He wrote many beautiful poems and loved this country very much. José Rizal was more than a poet"—Arturo's eyes glistened—"he was a hero. In the United States you celebrate George Washington—he is the father of your country, right? In the Philippines José Rizal is the father of our country. He paid a great price for leading our country to freedom. He rose up against the Spanish; he wanted freedom. He was executed by the Spanish. And so we celebrate this great man on December 30 by reading his poems."

I thought nothing could be more fantastic than to have a poet as a national hero, a man of words who was also a man of action and passion. Back home in Ohio I was constantly writing poetry. It was as if my mind could not think in straight lines, but in rhyme and verse. My teachers had tried to put a stop to it.

Once Papa came home from a parent-teacher chat, holding a stack of papers in his hand. "Poet"—for that's what Papa called me, his little poet—"Poet, your teachers say you are distracted, a daydreamer in class."

I hated school. I hated how everything had a time and place attached to it. This is algebra, this is history, this is penmanship. Watch your p's and q's, dot your *i*'s and cross your *t*'s. I was a poet.

Papa understood. He had handed me a notebook of lined paper. "Louise, here is a book for you to write in. Maybe you shouldn't write these things in class, but please, write them anytime you want at home. What you have is important," Papa said, waving the papers. "Don't stop. At school concentrate on the schoolwork. At home write all the poetry your heart and head can create."

When I reached the front porch of our cottage, a thin mist began to fall. The coolness on my skin refreshed me, helping me to feel better after such a heavy luncheon. I looked over the groomed lawn to the canopy of looming trees. In the distance I saw the sugar factories and then beyond them the fields of sugarcane. Far off I observed the blurred outline of mountains that split the island of Panay in half. Panay was ancient, formed by volcanoes erupting and melting away.

In the acacia trees I heard a rustling sound—probably some tropical bird stirring up the leaves. I walked over to the edge of the grove and waded into the thickness quietly, trying to not frighten the birds. Sparse droplets of water ran down my face and arms. All at once I heard the soft melodic voice of Melinda, our Filipino *lavandera,* or laundress. I pulled back the branches of a low-lying bush. Melinda was in the arms of her boyfriend, a worker from the cane fields. They were whispering and giggling to each other, trading kisses back and forth.

I silently let the branches swing back into place and ran for the house. Mother would never allow this, so I must keep Melinda's secret. I hurried upstairs to write poetry.

Lying in bed with my notebook open beside me, I thought about my life. The soft rain, the golden rim of sun coming through the clouds, the cove of damp trees, the warm kisses, the sweet smell of sugarcane coming up from the ground, the secret caves of the sea as the waves washed into them. I closed my eyes to better picture these driving images inside my head. I was adrift on a ferry, going from island to island. I was excited about the future, about paradise. A new world upon this ancient earth.

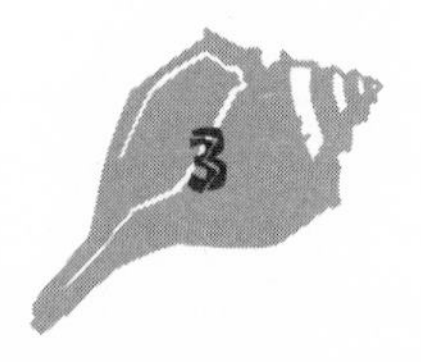

A Forbidden Dance

Being a Baptist was so boring. There was never anything to do—that is, anything I was allowed to do. Back home in Upper I had been invited to Sarah Jane Addams's fourteenth birthday party. It was to be a mixed party with both boys and girls from our eighth-grade class. Sarah Jane planned to play big band music on her new record player. Papa had forbidden me to go—it was on a Sunday afternoon. "Besides," added Mother, "Baptists don't dance."

I rolled my eyes and ran out of the room. It seemed that all my life I had longed to dance. The Methodist girls got to go to movies and dances. The Catholic girls got to wear pretty necklaces of saints around their necks, and in their purses they carried beaded strings called rosaries. How I wished I were a Catholic or a Methodist or something other than a Baptist!

When Julie called long-distance to Panay after we were there a few days, I was ecstatic. Her voice sounded so near, not halfway around the world. First Mother and Papa talked to her, answering questions about the trip and the weather. Then, before hanging up, they gave me a moment to speak with Julie. I wanted to pull her through the phone lines and look her in the face.

"Shakespeare?" she asked.

"Yeah, it's me, Julie. I miss you so much. What's new in Upper?"

"There's a really cute new boy at school. The senior class is sponsoring a dance Friday night after the football game, and I'm going. Maybe I can dance with the new boy."

Mother and Papa were standing at my elbow, hurrying me to hang up. I simply nodded into the receiver so as not to let on to my parents. "Good luck," I said. "Let me know how things turn out. Good-bye." The line crackled and I hung up.

Just two months ago, Julie and I had stayed awake talking. White moonlight flooded our bedroom, making the crisp September night seem almost like noonday. I looked out the window; the dew on the lawn dazzled and radiated.

"I'll miss you," Julie said, pulling me close. "Of course, I'll miss Mother and Papa, but I think I'll miss you the most. I'll miss talking about boys and movies with you. I'll miss playing hide-and-seek with you outside after dark. Everything will be different when you're gone."

I asked, "Do you suppose the same moonlight striking the ground here also shines in Panay? Maybe the moon you see at night will be the same one I'll look at over there." I gave Julie a big hug. "Think of me when you see the man in the moon. I'll be thinking of you. That way we'll always feel close to each other."

Julie smiled. "Tell me that in a year you'll be the same,

my Shakespeare, spouting poetry and full of crazy ideas."

"I promise"—I laughed—"to be crazier than ever."

Tears now stung my eyes. I didn't want to believe it would be another year until I saw Julie again.

I went upstairs and threw myself down on my bed. Across the room I saw my cardboard suitcase, slightly crushed on one side like the crown of a man's hat. I walked over and unpacked from the suitcase my magic seashell. Its luminous insides glowed, and I held it up to my ear just like a telephone to hear the waves. Deep calling to deep. I remembered back to another time on the boat crossing the Pacific.

I remembered the music of the ocean, the orchestra playing in the ship's ballroom, how I longed to dance. One evening after supper I lay in bed in our cabin, listening. Through the open porthole I could hear the orchestra tuning up. It was the oboes' turn to resonate, a sad and mournful song. I looked over at Mother, who was busy writing letters at a small desk. Her mouth was turned down and prim. It was as if she were thinking over and over, Baptists don't dance.

The walls of the small cabin closed in around me. I didn't want to live my whole life without experiencing sin; I had to escape. I told mother that I had left my sweater up by the deck chairs; I knew exactly where I had left it; I'd be right back.

Music from the ballroom wafted out through open doors. In the background I heard the tinkling of laughter and glasses. Shadows moved along the edge of the shuffleboard court. A couple emerged from the darkness, sipping champagne from tall-stemmed glasses. Unaware of my presence, the lovers threw their glasses overboard and embraced.

"I want to dance," I whispered to the night.

"Excuse me, what did you say?" I heard a smooth voice next to me.

I looked up and stared into the face of a tall man dressed in a black tuxedo with tails. His white shirtfront gleamed like moonlight reflected off the water.

"Uhmm... I said, Isn't it a wonderful dance?" My mother had soundly warned me against speaking to strangers, but everyone was a stranger.

"Where might you be headed?" he asked with a proper British accent.

I contemplated my mother's warning for all of two seconds. "To the Philippines. My father has taken a teaching position on the island of Panay."

"Really? I've been hired as a junior clerk in the national bank on the island of Cebu. There is a sugar refinery there and a great deal of commerce. I believe Cebu is just a hop, skip, and a jump from Panay."

This gentleman didn't seem much older than Julie. His blond hair stood out in contrast to his black suit. Immediately I became conscious of myself and my humble attire. I nodded in response.

"Allow me to introduce myself. I am P. B. Stuart. Recently from the banking firm of Carruthers, based in London."

"London—really, say, that's grand." I was lost momentarily thinking about London, England, and how far away that sounded.

"And who might you be?"

I blushed. "Oh, sorry. I'm Louise Keller and I'm from Upper Sandusky, Ohio. It should really be Lower Sandusky, because it's south along the river and actually below the bigger town of Sandusky, Ohio. . . ." I stopped, aware of how mundane Ohio must seem to this handsome world traveler. "Do I call you P. B. or Mr. Stuart?"

He smiled a half smile, a crooked smirk. "You may call me Peter, if you like."

A warm breeze blew across the deck. I was amazed at how comfortable I felt in short sleeves in the middle of October. "London must be a wonderful city."

"I'm actually from Manchester. The banking firm I am associated with is headquartered in London. I was sent out a couple years ago to do some clerking in Singapore. I'm working myself up the ladder of success by going to Cebu."

"You left London before the bombing, then?"

"They're having a rough time of it, I must say. I'm glad I made it out of there before the war started. I have no desire to be a soldier. I'd rather be fanning myself on the equator any day than marching around in the bloody squares with bombs dropping everywhere."

He paused a moment. "My father thinks I'm running away. While I was growing up, he talked endlessly about the Great War, the parades, girls kissing the boys good-bye. He was ruined by the war. In France he was blinded by the mustard gas. All I ever saw was an old man whose hands shook every time he took the bob out of his tea."

I felt uncomfortable listening to him speak so honestly. Behind us I heard a clarinet playing a familiar tune, "Moonlight Serenade."

Changing the subject, he continued, "A man can do well for himself in the P. I. if he can handle the heat and mosquitoes."

"But," I blurted out, "aren't you afraid of the cannibals and headhunters?"

Peter burst out laughing. "Bosh, what are you talking about? Maybe in the most remote areas, but not in Cebu."

I was thankful for the darkening twilight, which hid my burning cheeks.

"Before coming out, I spent over one hundred pounds to buy my kit—tailcoats, trousers, stiff shirts, cummerbunds, and cuff links."

"Why do you need all that?"

"There are garden parties and dances. I brought the whole regalia just on the off chance I may have to use it. As a bachelor I am expected to call upon all the senior bank officers and their wives."

"I've never been to a dance . . . I mean not yet, anyway." I tried to think of something else to say. "I found a shell. A perfect pink seashell."

He lit a cigarette, listening.

"Actually some fishermen gave it to me. And it's magic."

Peter picked a bit of tobacco out of his teeth. "Really."

"It has captured the sea. Storm and surf inside its pink petals. If you put it up to your ear, you can hear the ocean raging."

"That is magical." Peter turned his gaze toward the direction of another couple strolling on the deck. After a pause he said, "Good-bye; I hope to meet you again."

I nodded in agreement, feeling that our ever meeting again would be most unlikely since I didn't dance or frequent garden parties. He retreated farther down the promenade, and I sighed, resting my elbows on the ship's railing. After a second I glanced up and caught a glimpse of Peter staring at me with a funny smirk on his face.

I brought myself back to the present and put away the magic seashell. It was lonely without Julie. I imagined her dancing in a beautiful dress, her white teeth and bright eyes flashing. A small cry surged up inside of me; I wished for strong magic to bring us back together again.

At the beginning of December Papa left to go fetch the new schoolteacher and Freddy Urs from Manila. I quickly penned a letter to Julie and also included a letter to Sarah Jane Addams for Papa to take with him. The trip would take about a week, and we hoped that Papa would return with letters for us. I wanted to hear all the news from home.

4

Out of the Blue

Boom!

Something dropped. I heard a crash and hurried out of my room.

"Mother, are you okay?"

She was standing in a puddle of broken glass and cheap perfume. The smell of chemically created gardenias ripening through ninety-degree heat and humidity overwhelmed me. I thought Mother was upset that the bottle broke.

"I'm sorry, Mother. I'll help clean it up."

In the background a radio blared. "Once again, I repeat: The Japanese have bombed the U.S. fleet at Pearl Harbor. American lives have been lost and severe damage has been inflicted upon the fleet. We are still gathering reports and will pass that information on to our listeners as it becomes available."

Stunned, we waited in the stillness. Papa was in Manila picking up Freddy and the schoolteacher. In my ears was a low hum, a dizziness of too much perfume and bad news.

I was suddenly startled by the phone ringing. It was

Mrs. Urs. I heard her voice, magnified through the earpiece, shouting hysterically about the bombing. Mother handed the phone to me as if she needed an interpreter to translate the mad rush of choppy English.

"Yes, Mrs. Urs," I said. "We heard it too only a short time ago over the radio. . . . I'm not sure. . . . No. . . . I don't know. . . . Yes, I guess only God knows." It was more of a question than an answer.

I washed the floor, scrubbing the floorboards. I wanted to wash away the fears building up inside of me. I rubbed the wood until it seemed the varnish was coming off onto my rag, but the perfume smell remained in the cracks. I tried scraping with my fingernail, but the smell had permeated everything. There was nothing to be done but let it fade away.

At noon a report on the radio came from an English-speaking station in Manila. The Japanese had heavily bombed Clark Field on the main island of Luzon. Unbelievably, almost the entire fleet of planes had been hit. They were on the ground, waiting like ducks in a row for the Japanese to strike.

I tried to comfort Mother. "Thankfully, there were no bombings reported in Manila."

Her face blanched. "Don't even think that!"

Judson Smith and Mr. Albright quickly assigned themselves the duty of making sure the mission compound followed blackout regulations. In the tropics any light, no matter how small, was bright enough to attract attention from the sky. Tar paper, canvas tarps painted black, or thick layers of newspaper had to be tacked up at all windows before nightfall. It was a practical step to take our minds off the growing darkness and fear. We were at war with Japan.

The armchair generals, Smith and Albright, speculated on how long it would take to whip the Japanese and restore order in the P. I. Despite the discouraging reports of Japanese air attacks, they were convinced that within one hundred days it would all be over.

Mother tried unsuccessfully several times to phone Papa in Manila, but the island operator told Mother that all lines to Manila had been cut by order of the army. We found out the interisland steamers had been confiscated by the military; there was no way for Papa and Freddy to get to Panay.

Mrs. Urs fretted out loud, "I hope my Freddie is all right. Perhaps he is with your father. The new schoolteacher, too."

We heard a report a few days later that a plane was waiting at the airfield to take letters. Mother hurried to write Papa in Manila, and I wrote a quick letter to Julie, telling her we were all fine and not to worry—the war would be over soon. At least that was what Pastor Smith said.

I drove with Alice Gundry to the airfield in Iloilo City with our letters. At first glance everything in town appeared normal, but when I looked at the faces of people passing us on the sidewalks, I saw the fear. Nervous eyes looked straight ahead and tense jaws were set in hard lines. Alice and I stopped at a grocery store to stock up on some items, but the store was strangely empty. The only food left was a few cans on the shelves and four boxes of saltine crackers. We bought all there was.

As we were walking back to the car, we passed a bank.

Inside I saw tellers at little windows counting out pesos to long lines of worried customers. I thought about Peter, the bank clerk, and suddenly I had an idea.

"Alice," I said, thinking out loud, "don't you think that a bank might be able to get a call through to Manila? They have to have regular communications with their head banks all over the world. If not a telephone, then at least a telegraph."

"I suppose so. Why?"

"Maybe I could talk someone into letting me telegraph Papa at his hotel in Manila. I could leave a message for him that Mother and I are fine. He might be able to get a message back to us."

Alice, always the trouper, said, "Well, dear, it's worth a try."

We went inside. The difference between bright daylight on the sidewalks and the semidarkness inside the bank building almost blinded me. It took a minute for my eyes to adjust. I didn't want to wait in line, so I went to a side window and asked for the manager in a polite, small voice. I turned on all the charm of a young girl not quite fifteen.

An older man in a white suit introduced himself as an assistant manager. We told him our names and that we were with the Baptist mission. He invited Alice and me into a well-worn, untidy office where a Panama fan gently circulated the stuffy air.

"Please, sir," I started, "we are trying to get a message through to my father, who is at the Bayview Hotel in Manila. He went away almost two weeks ago to pick up our schoolteacher, and we haven't been able to get through to him. Can you help us by sending a telegram?"

I made sure there was a sweet whine to my voice.

"Now, missy, I am in no position to be sending frivolous telegrams through the wires. We have enough trouble getting all our regular business done to interrupt our transactions with a domestic matter."

I looked down into my lap. A real tear stained my dress. Alice handed me a handkerchief, and I blew my nose loudly.

"I think, perhaps," he began slowly, "since the Baptist missionary group does do a considerable amount of banking at this institution, we might be able to get one telegram through." I started up, excited. He continued, "Provided you keep it short and succinct."

"It goes to Reverend Arlen Keller at the Bayview Hotel." I tried to think of what to say. What was the one thing I wanted Papa to know? "Tell him all is well."

When I got home, Mother was still sitting at the table where she had written her letter that morning. Her coffee cup was empty, as it had been then. I wondered if she had moved. I put the boxes of crackers and the cans on the table and knelt in front of her. I was so proud of being able to get through to Papa when other efforts had failed.

"Mother, I have some great news."

She woke up as if from a dream and grabbed my arms so hard I thought they would break off.

"What is it?" she cried. "Is it Papa?"

"Yes, Mother. I was able to get a telegram sent out to him. I said we were all okay."

She stood halfway out of her chair, and then suddenly sat down. "Why, why"—she stumbled over her words, in a frenzy—"why didn't you bring back a message from him? That's what I want. I want to hear from him. Not *you*."

Mother burst into tears, shaking. Her coffee cup dropped onto the linoleum floor, exploding into a million fragments.

I stooped to pick up the bigger pieces. What once felt like victory had turned to disappointment. I wanted to cry but didn't dare. Something was happening to Mother, and without Papa here it was impossible to understand or to be understood.

Before I left to go upstairs, I said, "Mother, the sky was really blue today. Don't forget to cover up the glass on the front door. It'll be dark soon."

Rev. Judson Smith began wearing a uniform of khaki shorts and shirt, his skinny legs covered to the knee by black knit stockings. He marched around with a pith helmet, knocking on doors at dinnertime to remind all of us at the compound to keep our windows covered. Together Mr. Albright and Rev. Smith organized air-raid drills, instructing us all on where to take shelter in case of an emergency.

The letters we had written were returned undelivered. It was just a rumor after all about the plane; it had never left the airfield. Ann Fletcher carried the letters back to us.

"Y'all keep a stiff upper lip. We'll get through this thing, you'll see," Ann said, picking up Mother's hand and holding it. "There are so many reports—some true, some false. I don't know what to believe, but I've heard that Japanese troops are landing on Luzon." Mother didn't respond, but instead bit her lip and drew her breath in sharply.

Suddenly the air-raid siren shrieked throughout the compound. Without further warning, airplanes appeared in the sky—hundreds of them, low enough to the ground that a red dot was visible on the planes' undersides. The roar of motors overhead, combined with the piercing scream of the siren, sent Ann and me under the kitchen table.

"Mother, come on. Mother!" I cried. The air and light within the house were stifled by the planes' engines. I crawled back out and pulled Mother under with us.

Ann prayed, "Dear God . . . my babies . . . I left my children napping next door. Dear God!"

Her prayer reached a crescendo, and that was all we heard. The planes were gone. I rushed to the window. Thick smoke filled the air. I heard several small percussions and saw a burst of flames.

Judson Smith popped in through the back door. "We've been attacked!"

Ann pushed past Rev. Smith and headed next door.

"Can you tell us any more?" I asked.

"The airfield and the rail yard nearby were the primary targets. Everyone seems okay here." Rev. Smith looked around the kitchen. His eyes rested on Mother, curled like a snail beneath the table.

He helped me pull Mother out and get her seated. She wouldn't open her eyes. "Mother, they're gone. The planes are gone."

Ann returned. "The children are still napping." She shook her head in disbelief. "They don't even realize. I think y'all should move in with us until Mr. Keller gets back." Ann reached down and put her arms around Mother. A slight shudder ran down Mother's spine when Ann said Papa's name, but aside from that Mother never moved.

Ann must have read my thoughts: I was frightened at the idea of being alone with Mother in a dim and silent cottage. As I gathered my colored pencils and notebooks to put them into my cardboard suitcase, a photograph slipped out of one of the notebooks.

It was a picture of a Japanese schoolgirl. On the trip over, our steamer had docked in the port city of Yokohama, Japan. Mother and I toured the gardens of the city while Papa took time to cable Judson Smith in Iloilo with news that we would be arriving in Manila in less than two weeks.

In one garden a schoolgirl sat down beside us. Her braided black pigtails cut down her back. I smiled at her and she smiled back. I took out of my book bag a Kodak Brownie camera. Using hand motions, I indicated I wanted to snap a picture of her. She nodded yes, and I photographed her by a pool of swimming goldfish. Before we left the harbor, I penned a haiku, a form of Japanese verse consisting of only seventeen syllables.

The great pearl awakes
Fearfully I turn away
It is too precious

And now, the great pearl awakes and I am haunted by her face.

Sunrise the next morning, red through the ash. I carefully unrolled the tar paper from the window to look out.

Fire in the sky.
Red world dawning.

Suddenly, out of the blue
comes a warning:
Beware
of bombs and
fire in the sky.

"What are you writing?" Daisy asked, just waking up.

"A poem about the sky."

Daisy drew a picture for me using my colored pencils. "Here is Mommy and Daddy. Over there is Mae and you."

"What is this coming from the sky? It looks like black rain," I said.

"Not rain, Louise—bullets from the planes."

Mother volunteered to make a Christmas Eve dinner for the Fletchers. By combining pantries on the compound, everyone got a little bit of everything. We received a canned ham plus several cans of green beans, creamed corn, peas, yams, and baked beans. The compound would have to do without this year's Christmas barrel from the States.

To keep the girls busy, I improvised a Christmas tree using a potted lemon tree the Fletchers kept in their living room. "I wish we had garlands and lights," said Daisy.

"Now, Daisy, you know we can't have extra lights this Christmas," I told her. "Maybe we can make a garland, though. Let's see . . . what would make a perfect garland?" A month's ration of canned goods was lined up on the kitchen table. I had a brilliant idea. "Let's take the labels off and make a chain. They'll stay naturally curled without glue!" The girls worked busily while I told the story of the three wise men, and how they gave everything they had to buy precious gifts of gold, frankincense, and myrrh.

We wrapped the spindly lemon tree with our homemade label chain. "It's beautiful," whispered Mae, "just like the baby Jesus." She began to sing, very high and out of tune, "Away in a Manger."

We were still singing when Ann and Mother walked in. A smile spread across Ann's face as she gazed upon our Christmas tree. It was Mother who discovered the nude, unmarked cans.

"Louise, what have you done? You silly girl." She flew at me. "You've ruined these cans. How can I fix a proper dinner?" She began crying, her hands shaking in anger in front of me.

Ann took Mother by the shoulders. "There, there, Kate. Nothing is ruined. A little confusion, perhaps. Tonight we might have pork'n'beans and other surprises for our Christmas Eve dinner, but we'll be okay."

I felt humiliated. There was nothing I could do to please Mother.

In the midst of this scene Mr. Urs burst into the Fletchers' living room. "Come quickly," he shouted breathlessly, "it's Freddy and Reverend Keller on the telephone."

We ran over to the Urses's house. I made sure that Mother got to the telephone before me.

"Hello, hello, darling." Mother broke down crying. I pressed my ear to the receiver, listening in as Papa kept trying to reassure her that everything was going to be all right. His voice through the line sounded farther away than I wanted it to be.

"I got your telegram. It strengthened me to know you girls were all right." I was grateful to Papa for saying that.

"Tell Mrs. Urs that Freddie is okay. He's staying here

with me. I was able to get"—the line was crackling—"off the boat. She's with a missionary family here in Manila. The air-raid sirens wail day and night." More static. "I love you girls; be brave for me, will you. Poet, take care of Mom until I get—" The connection went dead; there was no more.

I helped Mother get back to the Fletchers', where instead of looking at Christmas lights we sat in a blackout watching the lighted dial of the radio. Our only link to Manila and Papa was the wireless, but at midnight KZRH and KZRM, both Manila stations, announced they were going off the air. Don Bell of Manila's KZRM, who always signed off with "Keep 'em flying," wept as he ended his broadcast. Our last connection to Papa was cut.

The sun rose bright on Christmas day, but I felt no sense of joy. Manila was nearly occupied; Japanese soldiers held most of the city.

Red world dawning.
Fire in the sky.

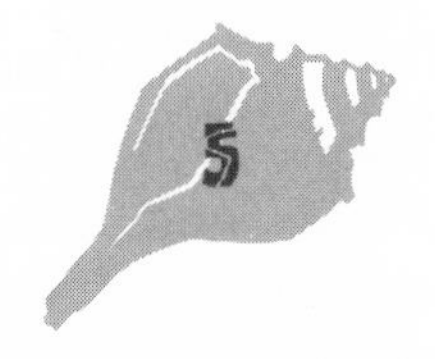

Into the Hills

Ever since the first bombing, Mr. Albright and Pastor Smith had argued over which type of air-raid shelter to build. Mr. Albright's plan was to build a shelter next to the house and camouflage it with sugarcane stalks. Pastor Smith contended that this was the stupidest idea he had ever heard. He knew for a fact that the dugout shelter was the best form of protection. He asked for all members of the compound to lend a hand in digging out a sizable shelter for one or two families. We needed at least three of these shelters shoveled out immediately. Mr. Albright thought that was a ridiculous waste of time. By the time such a shelter was built, we would all be dead. On and on the battle raged.

In the meantime Pastor Smith passed out gauze gas masks to everyone. A solution placed on the gauze prevented poison gas from suffocating the mask's user. The children were required to carry around their necks at all times a small piece of wood on a chain. In the case of an explosion, the wood should be placed inside the child's mouth to keep her mouth open and protect her eardrums from collapse.

What would have been unthinkable or shocking a month ago was now routine. Air-raid sirens, air-raid drills, blackouts, gas masks. Duck and cover. Holding out for rescue. Believing the best. Keeping a stiff upper lip.

I kept myself busy by teaching Daisy to read. She traced the alphabet in the sandy soil with her wooden stick. Mae wore her necklace proudly, the wooden amulet bouncing up and down on her chest as she skipped and played.

Bad news always seemed to come all at once.

From KGEI in San Francisco came the report that Singapore was under siege. The combined Philippine Armed Forces and the United States Army were on the retreat. The armchair generals, Albright and Smith, complained that President Roosevelt was selling us out—the war in Europe must be won first, then the war in the Pacific.

These days were like the foam that formed around the edges of the Sandusky River. During the summer, the river slowed, and at certain bends the water barely stirred, caught in a dead calm. In this eerie center were bits of leaves, twigs, and scum gathered into a thick soup. We were the brown, ugly foam that hovered before being swept away downstream.

To break the monotony, the girls and I planned a Valentine's Day party. Ann thought it was a great idea—"to get everyone out of their funk." Mother especially. Her spirits had risen so high after the phone call from Papa. She might have thought she was home, in Upper, and that at any minute Papa and Julie would walk in. But after Manila was bombed and the radio stations were turned off, Mother became as distant as Papa's thin voice stretching through the telephone wire.

Daisy and I addressed our invitations to Mother, Ann, Alice Gundry, Mrs. Urs, and Mrs. Albright. There was no colored construction paper, and I knew better than to pull labels off the tin cans again. Everything was saved these days. We saved the waxed paper and string from the grocer's. Tinfoil wrappers from chewing gum made decorative hearts for our invitations. With my pen I addressed penny envelopes inviting the ladies to join Miss Daisy Fletcher and Miss Mae Fletcher for a Valentine's Day tea party.

Mr. Albright, Pastor Smith, Mr. Urs, and Frank Fletcher were occupied with visiting the surrounding villages and had recently taken an extensive trip up into the mountains. I liked Frank. He collected bugs as a hobby. One night, just as twilight was coming, when everything was especially dark because of the blackout, Frank had pulled out his famous insect collection. With pride he shone a flashlight down on some of the most unnatural spiders, ants, and grasshoppers I'd ever seen. He bragged that he had close to four hundred identified species. The fragmented light exaggerated the bugs, lending them a weird, monstrous appearance. Odd angles of light multiplied the bug shadows against the walls. I shivered and congratulated him.

For the party Ann and I rolled out cookie dough and cut out a dozen heart-shaped cookies. After baking them, we sprinkled them with the last of the powdered sugar. In the P. I. sugarcane was the cash crop, and sugar processing the major manufacturing done on the islands. After such an abundance of sugar, it was hard to imagine going without.

Mrs. Albright, Mrs. Urs, and Alice Gundry arrived

around two in the afternoon. I was glad to see them wearing hats and gloves, just like old times. Mae served the cookies (with a little help), while Daisy and I served a terrific lemonade made from the lone lemon on the potted lemon tree. More than anything, the ladies loved being together.

We played a guessing game where each person had to guess who her secret valentine was. Taped to the back of each chair was a name. There was much laughter as we guessed and gave clues. Mrs. Urs was Eleanor Roosevelt. Mrs. Fletcher was the singer Dinah Shore. Mother was Joan of Arc. She carefully folded her name card in half. "Wasn't she burned at the stake?" she asked. Yes, but it was only a game.

Ann quickly changed the subject. "Frank and the other men have been scouting out the area inland. Can you believe it—hiking up to the mountains? They thought they might be able to make a camp for us in the jungles. We need a hideaway in a secluded spot just in case the Japanese should arrive."

"Will the Japanese actually get this far? Won't the American gunboats keep the Japanese off the island?" Mrs. Albright's face contorted in panic.

Mother flinched, gave a sudden twist in her chair. "My God, has it come to this, hiding out in the jungle like animals?"

No one in the room spoke. A quietness settled as the late-afternoon light slanted through the open tar paper.

Alice Gundry stood up and broke the silence. "It's the best idea I've heard yet. Let 'em come. We'll beat 'em. They'll be like cats chasing mice, and we'll wear them out looking for us up there. I say let the men build us a camp, and we'll be ready if the Nips come."

When it was time to go home, I overheard a few women congratulating Mrs. Albright. I asked Alice what everyone was so happy about. "I don't know about happy. Downright inconvenient if you ask me. Vivian Albright is going to have a baby."

After all the ladies left, Ann helped me clean up. "Thank you, Louise," she said.

"For what?" I muttered. I was still thinking about Mother. Why couldn't she have been Queen Esther and saved her people from doom? Why did I even write Joan of Arc down on a card?

"For many things. For entertaining my girls and letting them feel so grown-up today. Thank you for giving us back our lives."

I didn't understand what she meant. "Ann, what's wrong with Mother? I can't please her; I can't seem to make her happy."

Ann put her arms around me. "She needs you, Louise. Sometimes folks just run out of hope." I squeezed my eyes shut. "She'll find her way back. Things will be okay—you'll see."

The next day we learned Singapore had fallen—mighty fortress of Indonesia. We were brown foam clinging to the muddy bank, hoping the coming flood might not tear us apart. We lived each day prepared for a Japanese attack. Just in case, I had my suitcase packed with clothes and rations. Mother and I made over old clothes. I carefully pulled the hem stitches out of one of my dresses and sewed into it dollar bills—all that we had. Who knew how long until the Japanese came, and for how long we would have to hide out. I packed a satchel each for Daisy and Mae—a few outfits and a change of underwear in case there was no time to gather more and we must quickly retreat to the hills.

I asked Mrs. Urs why she didn't bother to pack. "Yah, thank God we are not at war; we will be safe." What was Mrs. Urs talking about? "Yah, Switzerland is a neutral country. We do not fight in this war. Japanese not make war with the Swiss."

All the colors—red, blue, green. I thought we were all blended together. I guess when the paper is about to go into the fire—well, maybe then the colors don't melt, but try to jump out. Don't burn me—I'm blue. I'm not involved here—I'm red. I resented Mrs. Urs and her Swiss neutrality.

One day Mr. Fletcher returned home mud-spattered from the trail. He had a long dirt streak on the back of his leg. After bathing, it remained.

"Here, sweetheart," offered Ann, "you missed a spot. Let me give it a wipe."

The streak stuck. It was a huge, blood-filled leech about two inches long. Ann screamed as Frank worked it loose and drowned it in a jar of ether.

"I'll add that one to the collection. A beaut."

At dinner Frank reported progress on our village in the hills. "The natives are helping out by building huts their way. High off the ground so the wild boars won't run through and smash everything."

Mother shuddered.

"The natives are really quite ingenious. They construct their houses on stilts. When the heavy rains come, the water runs underneath and hardly anything gets ruined. I

appreciate how the natives live. They can teach us a thing or two about how to survive in the jungles."

"Perhaps," suggested Ann, "we can make a trade—we can teach the women and children Bible stories in return for their backwoods know-how."

"I believe we will be getting the better end of the bargain," said Frank.

The Japanese were closing in. Mindanao, the southernmost of the major islands in the Philippine archipelago, was occupied by the Japanese. The Japanese had created a half circle of occupation stretching from Japan down through the Solomon Islands. With each new invasion, the Japanese mined that area's native wealth. From Java the army exported rubber back to Japan; from the Philippines they took back hemp for making ropes; from oil-rich Borneo they got fuel. Japan had all the materials for winning a war.

Japanese boats were reported to be off the shores of Cebu and Negros, neighboring islands to Panay. Warships not less than five miles out could haphazardly bomb the beaches with their cannons. We heard no news of real destruction—just a stirring of the surface, brackish foam shuddering.

Mrs. Urs was getting edgier every day about "the little yellow men." She was afraid of being abandoned when we all left to go off into the hills. She was a selfish, vain woman. From my bedroom window, through a small hole in the newspaper, I saw Mrs. Urs burying her silver one night. At first I didn't know what she was doing. Usually she left the gardening to Arturo. I saw her large bottom as she bent over and dug holes like a gopher. In the moonlight something shiny flashed. In one of the holes I saw her bury a teapot and in another a platter.

At breakfast the next day I mentioned seeing Mrs. Urs burying her silver. Ann shook her head. I knew she hated gossip, but she said, "Well, if you ask me, it's silly. Imagine—the only thing you think of saving, the one thing that has value—a silver teapot and plate. Our silver will rust, tarnish, and decay. That which is eternal has much more value in a time like this."

I wasn't sure Mother was listening. It had become her habit to sit for hours, expressionless, lost. She suddenly spoke. "I wonder what's going to happen to my subscription to *Sunday School Times.*"

"How's that, Kate?" asked Ann. It was good to hear Mother contribute to a conversation.

"My subscription to *Sunday School Times.* Do you think they are piling up on some dock in San Francisco or in a dead-letter bin? Perhaps after the war I'll get many issues at once."

Ann and I looked at each other. Mother was far away, reading her imaginary Sunday school papers.

Outside the house rain swept down like sheets blown about on a clothesline, gusting and then hanging straight. Through the walls I felt the wet fury. If only I could ride that wave of wind and water back over the ocean, stand on familiar ground, forget about the Japanese.

We celebrated my fifteenth birthday on the one hundredth day of war. On the same day, it was announced that Filipino boys escaping from Manila had come ashore in stolen sailboats. Frank and I went down to the beach to have a look-see. As it was early evening, we hurried over so that we could get back before curfew and blackout.

The boys were students no older than myself. I listened to their eyewitness reports. "We traveled close to the coast at night with only the moon to guide us. During the day we slept in sea caves. Japanese ships everywhere."

Manila was a ghost town, they told us. Many Americans had been put into camps and were held prisoner. The boys had seen Japanese troops parading captured American soldiers through the streets. Some Filipinos cheered; if they did not, the Japanese would retaliate.

One boy looked at me. "The Japanese are no good, very bad. They say they want to be the Filipino's friend, but they shoot Filipinos."

If the Japanese shot those whom they wanted to befriend, then what did they do with their proclaimed enemies? I looked out across the Visayan Sea. I imagined Papa a prisoner marching with a bayonet pointed at his head.

Frank escorted me home. No good. This one hundredth day of war—no good.

Cebu radio reported that U.S. soldiers had reached a point of no return—they had retreated to a tiny peninsula called Bataan. There was nowhere else to go except into the sea; the soldiers had to keep fighting for their lives until rescued.

Holy Week was approaching, and there was no way to celebrate traditionally by decorating eggs. Eggs of any kind were now an extravagance, costing more than anyone could afford to pay. There was an abundance of ripe avocados, though. As I gathered the huge green fruits, I was awed by their shape—elliptical like eggs. That's how I got the idea to color avocados instead of eggs. With wax crayons, the girls and I colored on the avocados. Mae drew little happy faces; Daisy spelled her name.

Arturo came by to observe our work. "Very pretty. Avocado good to eat."

"Yes; I found these on the ground over there."

"Be careful, missy—worms. Worms hide inside."

"Don't be silly, Arturo. They look wonderful." Wanting to change the subject, I asked, "Where is Bataan?"

He held up his hand and stretched out his pinkie finger. "This," he said, wiggling his little finger, "is Bataan, a little bit of land sticking out into the water. It means the 'place of children.'"

How could something so innocently named be the site of so much death and fighting? I wished Papa were here to explain.

On Easter Sunday, Pastor Smith preached from the familiar scripture: "I will lift up mine eyes unto the hills—from whence cometh my help. My help cometh even from the Lord." I searched the skies for signs of enemy planes.

Daisy and Mae sat in clean dresses for this special Sunday, their baskets of colored avocados resting in their laps. Suddenly the girls screamed. "Bugs! Icky bugs, Daddy!" Worms were crawling over the girls' pretty Easter dresses. Daisy and Mae jumped up, dropping their baskets to the ground. More worms burst out of the smashed avocados. I tried comforting the children while Frank quickly pocketed a few of the fluorescent green things.

Bataan fell. The soldiers could retreat no farther; they ran out of land and ammunition. Frank and the others quickly accelerated their efforts to move camp necessities out of the compound and up into the mountains; it was a race against the hourglass to get everything ready. With the help of hired porters they made weekly trips, taking in food, stoves, and building materials. No one could estimate how long we might stay in the hills.

Mr. Albright got into an argument with Frank one day. Frank insisted upon bringing his bug collection with him.

"Man, leave that behind. We can't waste time carrying useless boxes up the trail."

"I don't plan on leaving behind sixteen years' worth of work for the Japanese to spoil. Besides, last week you had us carry up your wife's sewing machine. My back is still smarting from that trip."

"A sewing machine is a useful piece of equipment. A benefit for the whole group."

"Explain that to my back." In the end I saw Frank pack his wooden cases into a trunk with extra bedding.

Finally zero hour arrived. KGEI reported that Cebu and Negros were occupied. The Japanese fleet was headed toward Panay. Our waiting had reached an end—we were off into the hills.

No Way Home

At the last minute Mr. and Mrs. Urs came with us. Frightened by the thought of living alone on the compound without God-fearing Christians, they overcame their neutrality. Of course, then it took twice as long to move our group to the base of the mountains. We had to leave behind most of the Urses' belongings since they had made no prior arrangements.

Most of the servants had fled. Only Arturo was there to say good-bye. Before leaving the cottage, I asked Ann about bringing Tiko, the parakeet. We needed all the room in the compound's car for people. "Let him go," she said. "The Japanese will never capture him." I released Tiko to the canopy of trees, the blue sheltering sky, the soft breeze.

Porters, or *mga kargador*, carried our bedding and suitcases for us. Mother insisted on carrying her wedding album. The trail started out flat in the sweltering humidity of palm trees, but hour after hour, switchback after switchback, we climbed higher and higher. Suddenly the sides of the trail fell off sharply into black, twisted ravines. After a dinner break spent clinging precariously to the wall of the mountain, we continued hiking, using vines as handrails. I helped to carry little Mae on my back while Frank carried an exhausted Daisy the rest of the way. Mother moved up the trail as if sleepwalking. Her eyes were focused straight ahead, as if disconnected from her surroundings. Dusk came quickly beneath the thick jungle foliage. By the time we reached our circle of huts, it was dark.

Frank proudly showed us how to climb the four-rung ladder up into one of the huts. Inside he lit a tin lantern. Light illuminated the walls, which were made from the fronds of the nipa palm. The floor was made of *sawali,* or split bamboo. Small carved hooks lined the walls, from which hung netted bags of food.

Ann looked around. "Well, I guess no one can accuse us of living in glass houses."

"No, I'm afraid not, darling. The worst that can happen to these walls is wind and mildew."

And monkeys, we learned soon enough. I shared a hut with Mother and Alice Gundry. That night we spread our bedding down like a mat right on top of the bamboo. Through a window cut out of the wall I saw the moon shine like a polished coin.

"I'm here, Julie." The light cut a path across the ribbed floor and walls. "Go, go and tell her and Papa where we are," I prayed to the moon.

After sleeping a few hours, I was awakened by screams in the darkness. The moon had climbed higher; it was hidden behind a rock outcropping. Mother shouted, "The Japanese are here! I saw a man standing over my bed!"

I quickly lit a lamp and looked out the window. I saw

a figure loping across the cleared grounds into the jungle. Frank and Pastor Smith arrived to check on what the commotion was all about.

"I think a monkey got in through your open window. We haven't got around to attaching shutters to all the windows," Frank explained.

Alice Gundry held Mother as she sank back down onto her mat.

Frank continued, "I tied some bananas up on one of the crossbeams, and I reckon the monkey was trying to get at them."

It was hard to sleep past sunrise in the jungle. Animal voices raised an ever increasing crescendo before dawn. A million birds recklessly called to one another. I awoke to a strange retching sound. For a moment I almost thought the monkeys had come back.

"Alice, what in the world is that awful noise?"

"I am eliminating bile." Alice leaned out of the window, spitting thick green phlegm. It was part of her morning routine to spend thirty minutes coughing and gagging and spitting.

I inspected the grounds that morning. There were four huts built up on stilts. Pastor Smith shared his hut with the Urses until one could be built for them. The Albrights and Fletchers each had their own tree house. Behind the camp was a cliff sheltering us from wind. Next to the stone cliff was a bodega, or storage hut, for our extra rations. To the west and south was dense jungle. The men attempted to separate the edge of camp from the jungle by laying a track of stones cleared from the jungle floor. Downhill was the river we had followed on our way up. It was from this river that we carried drinking water back into camp. In the center of the cleared area was the camp kitchen, which was open on all sides. Frank had improvised a barbecue pit and Dutch oven.

That first morning Ann prepared a breakfast from the jungle—fresh coconut milk, sliced bananas, and ripe avocados.

"We can live here forever off the bounty of the land," exclaimed Frank. "Why, I've already made a list of one hundred and one uses for our friend the coconut. It provides us with a milk substitute, its meat is food, and even the husks are useful in practical ways. With the center carved out, the husk can be a cup or a bowl, a scoop, or a kitchen utensil. If you're missing a button, I can carve one out of a husk. Dry husks can be fuel for the fire. Coconut oil provides light at night for our lanterns. Need a lift? Try coconut candy."

"Fletch, you've gone native," said Mr. Albright scornfully.

"Think what you will. We'll see who stretches their canned rations further—us or you. To my way of thinking, we should take advantage of God's blessings by eating the natural harvest around us."

During the day, my senses were awake to the smell of avocados rotting on the ground and the sight of the bright plumage of the zone-tailed pigeon. At night the sound of thunderclaps shattered the night sky, shaking the tin-can lantern hanging in our hut. This was my new life.

Frank and I planted a garden. He had already transplanted a few starts from our lowland garden and had brought with him several varieties of seeds. We experimented with the garden, taking into consideration the amount of sunlight the seeds would need, the amount of rainfall up in the mountains, and the mountain soil conditions. We'd plant a row, using a split bamboo thread for a plumb line and a stick for a hoe. We planted squash, peppers, lima and string beans, eggplant, peanuts, and corn. Frank tied the thin stalks of mountain tomatoes to a trellis. We also grew a native fruit called chayote, a pear-shaped squash with a very light taste.

Mrs. Urs laughed at the idea of a garden. "The war will be over soon. Who will harvest your garden, the monkeys?"

As we turned over the ground, we pulled out many large rocks and threw them to the side to arrange later around the property. "This is a magic mountain," Frank said.

"Magic? How's that?" I asked, pulling a three-inch worm out of the ground.

After a minute or two of examining the earthworm, we threw it, too, to the side. Then Frank answered my question. "These islands are all formed by volcanoes. Ages and ages ago they heaved themselves up out of the ocean. Earthquakes and underground explosions piled up volcanic rock until the Visayan Islands were formed."

I imagined fire and smoke spilling out of the sea. These rocky fields; steep, sloping ravines; and sharp, bare cliffs emerged from a passion way beneath me.

Our garden was secured by a strong *sawali* fence to keep out intruders. Frank suspected local pests such as rats and civet cats might plague us, so he rigged up an alarm system of tin cans and a cord. If a rat came mulling around, it'd get tangled up in the cord and rouse Frank with the clattering of cans.

One morning three village women visited the camp. The women were short, smaller than me, with stocky bodies and very dark skin. Their blouses were open to their waists, revealing large, drooping breasts. They spoke a greeting in the native Ilonggo language: *"Maayong aga"*—good morning. When their spokesperson opened her mouth, I noticed she had several teeth missing. The remaining teeth were little brown stubs.

Alice Gundry took the initiative to speak with them and translated their conversation for the rest of us. They brought news of the invasion. The day after we left Iloilo City, enemy ships were sighted along the coast. Philamerican forces, American and Filipino soldiers combined, retreated, leaving behind a path of destruction for the Japanese. Warehouses and bridges, oil tanks and rail yards, were set on fire. Many, many Japanese soldiers were on the island. It was likely that the compound was already occupied. The women explained that the village people of the mountains had begun to dig big holes in the mountainsides to trap Japanese soldiers if they came. The native women implied that they would protect our group and keep our camp a secret if, in exchange, we bought their chickens and eggs.

"I wonder what would happen if the Japs paid them more—would they tell anyway?" asked Mrs. Albright.

"Well, we'll be needing fresh meat and eggs. Let them bring their wares," said Ann. "We'll bargain with them then."

Alice Gundry gave them our answer. The head woman gave a broad brown smile. They went back up the steep trail winding into the cliffs.

• • •

The mountain women brought us our chickens. In addition they guided Arturo to our camp after assurances from him that he was a friend of the Americanos. We gathered around him, grateful to see a familiar face from the outside and hungry for news of the compound.

"Japanese very bad. They live at mission. They look everywhere for money. Broke door to Reverend Smith's office."

"They'll find nothing important. I buried most of the mission's papers in a steel-lined box in the yard," said Rev. Smith.

"Officers dig holes in yard looking for treasures."

I heard Mrs. Urs gasp.

"Is there any news from Manila?" I asked.

"No, missy. No way to talk to family. Very bad. At the bank in town, they fly Filipino flag upside down. Fly flag with big red mark now."

Arturo went on to tell of Japanese soldiers looting the warehouses, overrunning the plazas, and taking over the city. The roads out of town were crowded with refugees fleeing into the mountains for safety.

"They say all Americans and English must come down. They are putting people in camps. Many peoples together in camp right now. The school on the corner of General Luna and Mabini Streets is a jail. Many people taken there."

"It's true, then. Americans are being arrested and placed in prison camps." Mr. Albright shook his head.

Arturo was silent. Frank led Arturo to a sling-back chair and had him sit down. I brought him a mug of fresh limeade and papaya juice squeezed that morning. His hand trembled as he took the cup from me. Slowly he regained his strength. Soon his eyes wandered about the camp, taking in the huts and garden. "Very good garden. I stay and help my friends. I always help America—just like Huck Finn." I understood what he meant. He had supported us during the Spanish-American War and he would help us now. We were in this thing together, just like Jim and Huck. Hopefully, we would all escape to freedom like they did.

In the middle of the night I heard the alarm. The tin cans rattled and shook. A cat or rat sniffing around the garden, I presumed. I sprang up to look out the window. Down in the garden I saw Frank's outline slinking silently. He carried a bolo—a long machete knife.

Suddenly I heard a huge racket, the tin cans clamoring, and a loud snorting. Frank jumped back, startled, as a wild pig ran at him. His bolo dropped beside him. Wild pigs can be dangerous. They have a small horn in the center of their foreheads for goring their enemies.

I rushed out of the hut in my nightshirt, unsure of what direction to run in. I wanted to distract the animal away from Frank. Instead, the pig ran back toward him. By now the other men were outside shouting orders. The din confused the animal. Snatching up a blanket that had been left out to dry over some bushes, I made a sweeping pass at the charging pig. The weaving got tangled up in his horn, and he tripped. The pig went crazy, going nowhere madly. Frank whacked him with his bolo. I heard the pig scream under the blanket. Chasing the pig around the clearing, Frank kept whacking at it until the blood-soaked blanket lay down and died.

"Well, this certainly gives new meaning to the term pig in a blanket," Frank said.

In the moonlight, in their bloody pajamas, Frank, Arturo, Mr. Albright, Mr. Urs, and Rev. Smith gathered the ends of the blanket and dragged the wild beast down the path to the river. I followed behind. The nocturnal jungle was alive. Monkeys with their yellow eyes looked down at me; fruit bats hovered above the overripe avocado trees like gnats.

At the river's edge, Frank slit the pig's belly with the bolo. A stinking bile flushed out. The men continued cutting, pausing occasionally to wipe the blood from their knives. Frank had been raised on a farm down South and knew how to butcher a hog. It was hard work hacking and sawing, but eventually, by the time the sun was easing the moonlight pale, they had a pile of meat cut up.

The next day Ann, Alice, and Mrs. Albright began smoking the meat, using the charcoal fireplaces and spits. Mrs. Urs cut a slice from the shoulder; grease ran down her fingers and arm. She smiled up at Mother. "*Gutt,* very *gutt.*"

Travelers on the trail often stopped by. Frequently we saw groups of stranded soldiers zigzagging up and down the mountain switchbacks. I was down at the river's edge one day filling buckets of water for the camp. A patrol of guerrillas shifted out of the shadows, cautiously approaching the stream. The soldiers wore ragged army castoffs. One man wore only a loincloth. I could smell their sweat.

"*Maayong aga,* good morning. My name is Louise Keller."

"Hello," said one of the men, an American in civilian clothing. "My name is Ward Gunther. We've been out trekking for a couple of days. We've heard your camp caught a pig."

I invited the men into our camp. We were desperate for news; reports from the lowlands came slowly. Those of us hiding in the mountains received typed-out radio reports from the inland city of Passi several days after the reports were broadcast.

"Corregidor is holding out," Mr. Gunther proclaimed. Corregidor was an island guarding the mouth of Manila Bay, a rock fortress with a system of underground tunnels. Nothing could penetrate that base. "The strategy is to fight long enough to waste the Japanese bullets and bombs."

Mr. Gunther had managed an oil refinery in Iloilo City before the invasion. He and his wife, convinced an attack was coming, had planned ahead and built a camp about four miles north of ours.

"We brought out Mrs. Gunther's piano. You must come join us for a concert. Consider this an invitation to hike over and see us sometime."

I offered the soldiers a slab of our roasted pig. They smiled in appreciation, grabbing at the strips of meat. I noticed that one of the men had trouble eating. His hands were bruised, the nails on his fingers mottled blue and yellow. He smiled nervously at me and continued eating.

After their meal they continued on the path. I asked Frank about the native's fingernails.

"The poor man was tortured, no doubt, by the Japs. They drive slivers of bamboo under the nails to get prisoners to talk, to reveal guerrilla headquarters and hideouts."

I shivered in the bright sunlight. At times it was easy to

forget there was a war going on, but at other times the reality filtered through, and then everything came sharply into focus.

A trip to the Gunthers' hideaway was organized. The travel party consisted of me, the Fletchers, and Alice Gundry. At first the trail was steep, dug into the side of the mountain. As we wound higher and higher, using the switchbacks, we eventually noticed a gentle sloping. Soon we entered a rain forest made up of huge trees with trunks the size of cars. Tilting my head backward, I looked up into the treetops. They were the earth; they were the sky.

Beside the path we saw several kinds of vines growing among the trees. One vine with long, narrow leaves and fragrant, star-shaped flowers, white with yellow centers, circled a tree, spiraling high up into its branches. Another vine clung tightly to the tree trunk; it had flat, spread-out leaves and flowers shaped like miniature saxophones.

The trail dropped suddenly, forcing us to descend by holding on tightly to roots jutting out. At a river's edge we took off our shoes and stockings. Frank went first, carrying a rope that he had tied to a tree. Once across, he tied it to a sturdy root. The rest of us followed, using the rope as a banister. The rushing stream whirled around us, but we were never in any real danger of being swept away.

After resting a little, we continued our hike. Ahead were bare, rocky fields and patches of tall cogon grass. At long last, the path wound down to a lake nestled in what had once been the crater of an active volcano. The Gunthers' house was situated on the very edge of the lake—a perfect hideaway. The walls were made of hand-hewn logs, still covered with bark, and the roof was thatched just like that of an English cottage.

"It really is quite a place you have here," Frank said to Mr. Gunther as we reached the yard. "I think you could live off the land here for two or three years easily."

"Well, we had plenty of time to build it. We're in the process of building a second evacuation home higher up still. I see the Japs flying overhead trying to spy out mountain camps. They'll eventually come looking for us, and when they do, we'll move on."

Helen Gunther came out of the front door. She was a small woman, sophisticated and charming. I noticed right away that her nails were painted an almost clear pink. More than likely she had once been used to garden parties, country clubs, and fancy hotels. Nevertheless, she didn't seem out of place in that lovely clearing.

Mr. and Mrs. Gunther prepared a feast for us—grilled carabao (water buffalo) steaks and a salad made from several kinds of greens topped with avocados and wild mushrooms.

"Yum, these taste just like home fries," Ann said, digging into a bowl of what looked like potato chips.

"Yes," said Mrs. Gunther, "those are fried green bananas sliced real thin. Aren't they delicious?"

After dinner Mrs. Gunther served coffee and coconut pie. The crust was soft and flaky; it was just like a pie from Miller's Bakery at home. While relaxing, Helen played the piano that had been brought all the way up from Iloilo City. The tinkling sounds overlapped with the rhapsody outdoors—birdcalls blended with the high-pitched cheep of the monkeys, an orchestra of the islands.

Before going to sleep, we tuned in KGEI on the radio. It was much better to listen to the news firsthand than to read the typed reports a day or two later.

"Corregidor has fallen," said the announcer. Our last hope was now gone. General Wainwright had surrendered to the Japanese. All troops were ordered to lay down their arms and offer no more resistance to the Japanese. The report went on to say that General MacArthur had arrived in Australia after secretly leaving the island, apparently abandoning us. We felt forgotten by our own country. The heaviness of the meal shifted in my stomach. The Philippines were completely in Japanese hands.

I stepped outside into the chilly night air while the others continued to talk in hushed tones. Overhead the sharp stars sliced the night sky close to my face. I clasped my arms about my shivering chest.

After a few weeks, a new group of women visited our camp. They wore native costumes of transparent cloth made from the fibers of the pineapple leaf—almost like linen. Their blouses were a loosely woven net that exposed brightly colored undershirts, some beautifully embroidered with bright thread. For skirts they wore patterned sarongs tucked around their waists.

They brought with them a three-page typed report from KGEI. The U.S. Navy, crippled after Pearl Harbor, had managed to defend a tiny island near Hawaii called Midway, turning back the Japanese fleet. American and Australian bombers were hitting the Japanese in New Guinea, and Doolittle was flying raids over Tokyo. In Russia, the Germans were again on the offensive, driving toward Stalingrad. British RAF planes were over France and Belgium, while Cairo reported activity along the Libyan front. U.S. soldiers were stationed in Iceland and the Aleutian Islands of Alaska. The Japanese were encountering heavy resistance in Burma and South China.

Where was there no war? Was there no place on this planet immune from fighting?

One of the women spoke a little English. She was a nurse who worked in a hospital in Passi. Her brother was a soldier in the Philamerican army. She worried about him being sent to a prisoner-of-war camp.

The women gathered around Mrs. Albright, who was almost five months pregnant, speaking to her in singsong voices and patting her tummy. Mrs. Albright nervously stepped away.

"You have baby soon," the nurse translated for the women. "I come back and help you get baby out. I help many baby come."

"No, I want to go to a real hospital," replied Mrs. Albright. I could tell she didn't like the native women touching her.

"Japanese take over hospital in Passi. No go to Passi to have baby. Very dangerous."

"I'll have my baby in a civilized hospital," Mrs. Albright said, her jaw set hard. "I will." She sank down on the wooden steps leading up to her hut.

Ann sensed her frustration and sat down next to her, rubbing her back. "Of course you'll go to the hospital. We aren't in any backwater swamp, no cotton picker's patch. We'll get you the best there is."

The women talked on, and Alice Gundry translated. "They say it is a custom . . . that a child will always find his way back . . . learn the way . . . home . . . if the mother buries . . . the afterbirth outside the house."

Mrs. Albright couldn't bear the discussion any longer.

She cried out, "How disgusting! Please, Alice, make them go away."

In June, the dry season, the insects were at their peak. An abundance of bees and butterflies pollinated the orchids. One butterfly in particular had Frank and me baffled. Each time it passed a plant, without perceptible pause it deposited a tiny yellowish egg, until as many as ten or twelve were left sticking to the surface of the chosen leaves. We observed the larvae hatch and begin their life struggle, but invariably they died or disappeared before passing one or two molts.

Frank's ant collection was packed away in metal boxes hidden in the hollow trunk of a tree near his nipa-frond shack. When we came up the mountain he had about four hundred identified insects, one hundred of them new to science. In two months he had added ten new species. One discovery was very unique, a mutant. The ant had two pinkish-white heads, both connected to a white abdomen. Frank named it Ananias and Sapphira.

"Ach, how can you look at such things? They are disgusting."

Mrs. Urs sat on the ground beside a garbage heap of rusting tins. The whole time on the mountain she had been an aggravation, fighting over the most trivial of matters. She believed she was always right.

"Today I dreamed we were leaving this place," she said. "What I dream always comes true. You'll see."

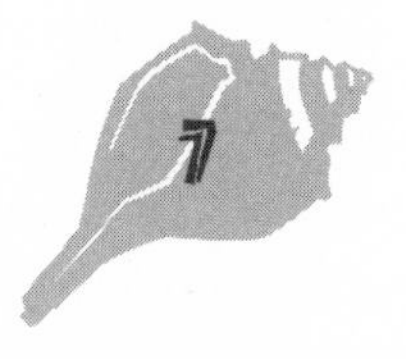

Christmas in Captivity

June 21, 1942

Dear Julie,

I know this letter will never get to you. We are prisoners of war. Mother and I are at a camp in Iloilo City at the primary school. Papa is in Manila, but that is another story.

We had gone up into the mountains to hide. We lived there quite contentedly for a few months, until one afternoon we were just getting ready to sit down to our lunch and the Japanese burst into our camp. Seven soldiers pointed their guns with bayonets at us and spread out like a fan to look for more prisoners. Frank had been out cross-pollinating an orchid when they arrived. I saw him hiding in the thick vines beyond the rock border of our camp.

"The game's up, Frank. Come on out," Ann called.

The Japanese searched our belongings. They took our toothpaste. We didn't have much time to pack—just a small bag and nothing else. I remembered to bring my poetry books and several notebooks. I hope they will let me keep these.

Mother cried only once while moving down off the mountain. "Oh, my God," she moaned, "I've left my wedding album up there." She rocked back and forth in the open truck, but no tears came. Frank left behind sixteen years of field research in a hollow tree. He'll go back for it someday.

All the days and weeks of waiting were wrapped up in a few brief minutes. All the wondering, what-ifs, and worrying came down to this—we are prisoners and free no more.

I love you,
Louise

Heat rose up to meet us. After the cool nights spent on the mountain, we sweated in the sweltering, wilting humidity of the barracks. The men slept at one end of the school building, while the women and children stayed at the other end. Families were together during the day and at meal times, but at night they parted.

Mother and I shared a classroom with about ten other women and children. Bedrolls, mats, and some cots lined the walls, with a narrow aisle in the middle of the room for walking. There was no place to go, no place to be alone.

"Living piled up on top of one another in everyone else's business" was how Ann described our new situation.

Arturo and Mr. and Mrs. Urs were forced to stay at the mission compound without us. Our Japanese commandant said, "Japanese no make war on Swiss peoples." Mrs. Urs visited us every week, bringing little packages of food and toiletries.

The Japanese required all enemy aliens to register. I went with Mother to a classroom that served as the commandant's headquarters. As I walked into the room, I saw Japanese soldiers standing at attention with bayonet rifles; fear filled me. I had to do all the speaking. Mother wouldn't answer, couldn't. I was hesitant to speak for fear I'd be taken away and tortured. I had heard stories of men who were taken for questioning and returned badly beaten. There was no way to know how the enemy's mind thought, what insignificant slip of the tongue might be twisted into an incriminating confession.

The commandant, Mr. Yano, was actually a Japanese civilian who worked for the Japanese army, but he made it clear he was our superior.

"Your names," he demanded. "Ages. Where are you from?"

I answered for both Mother and myself. "Ohio."

A look of quick recognition crossed Mr. Yano's face. I repeated, "Ohio."

"Yes, yes, but where are you from?"

I ran my fingers over my lips, trying to think. What if *Ohio* was a secret code word? Would I be dragged away and fed to the rats or returned in the back of a truck like Mr. Henry, an older gentleman accused by the Japanese of dismantling machinery at the local shipyards after the invasion? He came back with bruises and cuts over his face, arms, and legs.

I spoke again slowly. "Ohio."

The guards around us broke into smiles. "Ohio, Ohio, Ohio," they all echoed.

We were excused from further questioning. Frank told me later that the Japanese thought we were being polite. "*Ohio* sounds like their word for *hello*."

Thank God we got off on the right foot. Others were not quite so lucky. Mrs. Morrow, a British woman whose husband was in the exporting business, spoke out one day during morning roll call.

"Mr. Yano, I need to have a word with you." She stepped forward without bowing. She was a tall, big-boned woman. Mr. Yano had to look up at her. "The camp needs water. The water tanks provided for us are old and rusty. The water the men must fetch every day simply leaks out onto the ground. You've given us rice, but no firewood. How do you expect us to cook the rice with no fuel or water?"

Mr. Yano's eyes narrowed with anger. He reacted to Mrs. Morrow's request by quickly slapping her with the broad side of his hand. Those of us standing at attention muffled our shock at seeing a woman struck by a man.

"You are a very proud woman."

Mrs. Morrow returned to her place in line with a red handprint lingering on the side of her face.

On Thanksgiving Day 1942, I sat on the verandah that wrapped around the school building. It was the one spot to sit where I could see over the wall surrounding the grounds. That day I saw Japanese soldiers dismantling a small bungalow across the street. They methodically removed the corrugated metal roofing, being careful to save even the nails. Next they stripped off the gutters, beams, walls, and window frames. The removal of the bungalow brought into clearer view the city garbage incinerator. I saw its smokestacks puffing away.

I shook my head and looked down at my faded dress

and mud-spattered feet. I wished there was one thing I could be thankful for. I was glad there were no more air-raid drills or bombings, but on the other hand we were prisoners. I was happy Mrs. Albright had had her baby. A healthy girl, but Rose was colicky and kept everyone awake at night with her incessant crying. I liked being able to spend more time with Daisy and Mae, but there were no other teenagers on the place who understood or felt the same way I did.

I closed my eyes and thought in despair, From whence cometh my help?

When I opened my eyes, there was Mrs. Urs approaching the fence with a package. She bowed to the guard, and the guard motioned me over to the fence.

"Today is your Thanksgiving, so I give you a little something extra." Her voice dropped so that the guard wouldn't hear. "I talk to Freddy. He says he is safe at Santo Tomás, a camp in Manila. He stay and take care of your father. Mr. Keller was ill with a fever." A look of panic crossed my face. Mrs. Urs quickly continued, "But he is better now. He is getting adequate care, my Freddy tells me. My boy, he wants to stay a prisoner, stay with Mr. Keller."

"This is indeed good news, Mrs. Urs. Thank you for the extra 'package.'"

"Yah, the Japanese say we are free to go, maybe to Argentina, but I cannot leave like other Swiss."

I watched Mrs. Urs go. I didn't always understand Mrs. Urs or agree with her, but without her help we would have suffered terribly.

Our Thanksgiving meal was a banquet for poor, hungry eyes and also a feast for our empty stomachs. When we entered the small cookhouse, we discovered a turkey on a platter. Our "turkey" was a large squash called a *camote,* something like a sweet potato. This *camote* was naturally shaped like the torso of a turkey. The neck was the stem. Long bananas fastened on with a copper wire stuck out like legs, and the turkey's wings were made of slices of *camote.* Surrounding the "turkey" on a platter were red beans and rice, which looked almost like dressing.

The *camote* turkey was just a centerpiece. There was real meat with vegetables and fruits, donated by friends outside of camp. For a week the women had cooked over an open fire in the afternoons, preparing one thousand pieces of chocolate-coconut fudge so that each of the 146 internees could take several pieces back to their rooms.

Mother and I ate on the verandah with Ann, Frank, and the girls. It was the closest I'd felt to home in a long time.

December marked the anniversary of the bombing at Pearl Harbor and the end of the first year of war. Our Japanese guards celebrated by getting drunk on saki (rice wine). We watched from the verandah as they sang strange, garbled songs and threw their empty bottles through the school windows. A woman on her way to the privy was patted on the bottom by one of the guards. Among the internees there was general outrage.

"Just let that Nip touch my behind, and he'll get what's coming to him." Alice shook her fist at the fence. Alice could take on the entire Japanese army and have them come out smarting over their wounds.

Later that night Ann, Alice, and I talked in whispers before going to bed. "You know they think they are better than us," Alice said.

"Well, they should. They have us like a fox in a henhouse," retorted Ann.

"No, what I mean is that it's their religion to see themselves as superior. Godlike. They believe they are descended from gods and that their emperor is God. Not like our God, you understand, but a divine being. Anyhow, it's what makes them do those crazy dances so early in the morning."

It was true. Before the sun rose, our Japanese guards lined up outside our schoolroom, wearing only thin loincloths. In this manner they greeted the rising sun, chanting and performing a ritual by slowly moving their arms and legs. It was said they were committing themselves to their emperor and to Nippon, the ancient name for Japan.

"God grant that they shouldn't be too good warriors," Ann said, blowing out our tiny candle lamp.

Christmas Day arrived—my second in the Philippines, my first in captivity. It came without store-bought presents, without Papa, Julie, or Mother. Mother mostly lay in bed except for when I took her by the hand and led her to the shower, the toilet, or to meals. She had hardly spoken a word since her outburst about the wedding album. As I looked into her vacant face, I often wondered what she thought about. Was she thinking of Papa? Without Papa she was missing her other half, the part of her that said she fixed good meals, thanked her for being a good wife, held her hand, and smoothed her hair at the dinner table. It was hard watching her crumble a little bit more each day.

I busied myself by making Christmas presents for the girls from materials available inside the camp. I made

Daisy and Mae their own little tin cups from condensed-milk cans. First I rounded the rough edges of the tops by heating the tins over our cook fire and pounding the edges with a rock. Next I soldered handles to the cups and with a nail engraved their names.

Mugs were essential to camp life. Into our mugs went carabao milk or hot soup for the children, thin coffee or hot water for the adults. Everyone's original cutlery and plates had broken long ago. Internees fashioned their own cups out of coconut husks or tin. The coconut husks tended to be a little uneven, thus tipping the hot soup. Tin rusted after long-term exposure to hot liquids. We were constantly replacing cups and bowls.

I thought long and hard about what to give Mother. She didn't need a new cup or bowl. I knew what she wanted, and I couldn't get it for her. It was Papa, far away in Manila. How could I get Papa? I wished there was some way to surprise her with the one thing she needed most.

Christmas morning after roll call, before we all dispersed to open presents and prepare a special meal, I approached Mr. Yano. I knew he had the authority to punish me for approaching without permission, but it was a chance I had to take. With his hand he could slap me, spank my bottom in public, or send me away in a truck.

"Mr. Yano, please, sir."

I fell down flat, prostrate before him. I heard Ann mutter, "Oh, my goodness, what is she doing?"

My extreme act of submission surprised and apparently pleased Mr. Yano. He gave me permission to stand. "What is it that you want?"

"I am here with my mother from Ohio." I wanted him to know we were a friendly people. "My father is at the

Santo Tomás internment camp. My mother and I wish to transfer to that camp to be with him."

Mr. Yano smiled a broad, open grin. His white teeth flashed. "No need for this. War over soon and you will all be together."

Just like in a game of musical chairs, I was left standing without one. I reproved myself—I had nothing to give.

Before lunch, I took Mother for her shower. "Mother," I said, squeezing an old rag out on her back. The gray soap film slid down her bony spine. "Won't it be great when we see Papa again? He's at Santo Tomás," I reminded her. She flinched slightly; the nerves in her neck tightened up. I guided her back to our room, where I dressed her and tied her shoes.

Daisy came into the room shouting, "Santa Claus has been here after all." She waved an old mended sock in the air. Inside her stocking was the tin cup I had made for her and a gift from Mrs. Urs—cardboard stars decorated with green wrapping paper with the words *Merry Christmas* in cursive gold lettering. Frank had carved the girls darling little rings from carabao bones.

"Merry Christmas, Louise." Ann came up behind me to give me a hug.

A lump stuck in my throat. "There is nothing for me. What I want can't fit into a stocking. It isn't here." I broke down crying.

"You're a very brave girl. You're doing the best you can taking care of your mama. Louise, I know our heavenly Father will provide for you. He will bring you out of here. There will be an answer, and deliverance will come."

"Oh, how can you be so sure?" I pulled away and went outside to sit down on the verandah.

Ann followed me outdoors and sat on the steps beside me. "Let me tell you a little story. A Christmas story.

"My people were poor; I didn't expect much at Christmas. My father was a preacher. He liked to tell people about the year of Jubilee. You know what that is, Louise?"

"I think so. Isn't that in the Old Testament? When slaves were freed and their debts forgiven."

"That's right. A time when the poor would have plenty. My daddy rarely ever got paid in money. Always with a sack of something. A sack of pecans, a bushel of apples. People brought these things when they could. It'd make me so mad. I always wished they'd bring us something really good."

I understood her there.

Ann was lost, telling her story. When talking about home, her Southern accent came out with every word.

"I remember one night. Seems I was your age and always starving. You can only get so far on bread, pecans, apples, and other people's handouts. One night a man came with a lantern, telling Daddy to come down to the Gulf. We didn't live too far from the Gulf, where the warm waters come up from Mexico. Daddy took me with him, since I was the oldest. By the time we got to the shore, we couldn't see the water, there were so many people. Dead of night and a hundred people standing at the water's edge holding lanterns, like fireflies up and down the coast. I came closer and saw folks were scooping up fish. Something about the moon and warm waters had messed up the fishes' sense of direction. A freak of nature. They were actually swimming into our nets! You could put your hand down and they'd come up just like a stray dog to be petted.

"My pa called it a Jubilee. Folks around us were almost spent—no jobs, no work, no food. Nothing to hope for. Then this harvest came in. All night long folks were cooking the fish over open fires or salting them and laying them out on logs to dry. Some took them home and pickled them. It was one night and then no more. We lived off those fish for six months, and I suppose other families did the same. It sustained us through the hard times.

"I always remember how God gave to us at just the right time. In the year of Jubilee he will provide. Keep this in mind. Be strong for your mama. She isn't like you. She can't remember a time of harvest right now."

I thanked Ann for her story. I wasn't sure about the Jubilee, but one thing I knew: If by some miracle or luck the tide actually ever came in, I'd have the misfortune to be drowned.

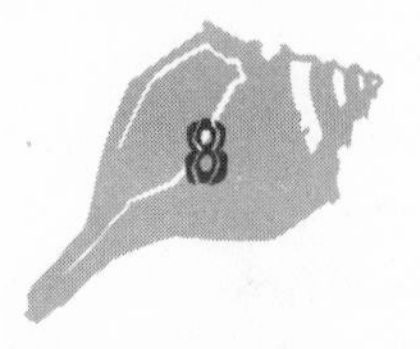

THE SAME DAY, DAY AFTER DAY

JANUARY 1, 1943—a new year and a new group of prisoners arrived. Every week internees were being rounded up and brought in. Among the new internees was a pretty girl a little bit older than me, about Julie's age. She had come out right before Pearl Harbor to join her boyfriend on Panay. He worked at the docks, but when war was declared he went off to fight. He was with the American forces on Mindanao, and she had not seen or heard from him for months. She didn't know if his troop had surrendered or was still resisting somewhere in the jungles.

I introduced myself and offered her a piece of leftover Christmas coconut fudge.

"Hi," she said, "my name is Marty. I came out from Oklahoma to marry my boyfriend, John. Thought I'd make a clean start, and now look at me—I could have stayed home on the farm instead of being penned up here like a dog. I traded one prison for another."

I agreed. "I'd much rather be stuck in a small town than be bowing to Japanese guards." I crossed my eyes and did a small curtsy. We both laughed. It felt good to talk with someone close to my own age.

A Catholic priest also arrived with the group. Originally from the Netherlands, Father Jan had come over forty years ago to serve in a leper colony in Antique. Because of the war the colony was completely cut off from its food supply. Father Jan and the lepers had tried to escape from this remote area of Cebu by sailboat.

"There were seventy-two of us. We drifted for days off of San José, but the Japanese would not give us permission to land. Instead they opened fire on our little boat. Most of us were wounded or else drowned in the sea."

Father Jan paused, pulling in his dry lips. "The Japanese soldiers kept shooting their machine guns into the water. They did not want the lepers." Tears filled his eyes. "I managed to escape onto some rocks off the coast. Bodies washed up beside me. And then that night there arose out of the sea an octopus. She was sleeping under the ledge. I disturbed her beauty rest and she came after me. Got me here," he said, pulling back his robe and rolling up his trousers. He pointed to huge red welts on his calf. "The Japanese bullets got the octopus, but not me—I'm still alive." Father Jan patted his chest.

I shook his hand. "I'm so glad you made it, Father." His handshake was strong, filling me with courage. If Father Jan could defy bullets and defeat sea monsters, then I could overcome my dreary imprisonment.

The camp celebrated the New Year with an old-fashioned game of American baseball. Never mind that half the internees were not American. It was fun to see the Brits batting the ball with total disregard for the rules. Father Jan added to the confusion by hobbling from first base to third, entirely skipping second base. Mr. Albright ran out onto the field yelling about procedure and point-

ing to second base. Father Jan merely laughed and kept on running.

Every day we lived with some new rumor—our guards were going to kill us, we were leaving the island for another internment camp, Mussolini was on the run in Africa, Hitler had been assassinated, President Roosevelt had thrown in the towel. It was all so mixed up and confusing. A lot of energy was spent on worrying about false information and trying to learn the truth.

Each day passed as routinely as the day before. We were hot, tired, and afraid. Special days were few and far between. For my sixteenth birthday Marty made a dress over for me. She was very handy with scissors and thread. She actually had been able to sneak several copies of the *Ladies' Home Journal* into the camp. I pored over the magazines at night, looking at the ads for makeup and new clothes.

"I can make a pattern out of just about anything. If I see something once, I can turn around and whip it up out of a burlap sack," Marty bragged. She had been raised poor on a farm and had a huge case of the "I wants."

"I sure do miss my man and his loving arms," Marty continued dreamily. I had never been allowed boy-talk at home. Mother disapproved of her girls acting silly about boys. Mother had a strict Baptist upbringing by her aunt Beatrice after her mother, my grandmother, died of tuberculosis. Aunt Beatrice was the worst sort of Baptist. I'm sure Aunt Beatrice had no trouble avoiding dances, card games, and movie houses.

On certain evenings movies were shown in camp—scratched-up silent films projected upon the white walls of the classrooms. At home I was not permitted movies. They were considered sinful. But here at Iloilo there was no Aunt Beatrice, and no Mother—or at least no mother who noticed much of what I did. War had upset the balance of good and evil; nothing made sense. I concluded that all the Baptist rules in Ohio didn't amount to a hill of beans in Iloilo.

On Sundays our Buddhist guards gave no roll call; it was my only day to sleep late. Ann insisted that I attend church.

"We cannot forget our Christian responsibilities. There might not be a house of God on the grounds, but at least we can still assemble together as true believers."

The card table used throughout the week for bridge games was converted into an altar for Sunday services. The Protestant service took place between two Catholic masses, one in the morning and one in the evening. I asked Ann if I could attend the later mass.

"No ma'am. You might think you're smarty-pants enough, being sixteen and all, but you ain't old enough yet to change your religion."

I rebelled in a small way by signing up for choir rehearsals with Father Jan. He was planning a performance of Handel's *Messiah* for Easter. Marty joined the choir, too. She had no real religious convictions, but thought a boy from the camp might be joining.

"Marty, what about John?"

"Well, John is John. I like him well enough, but Bob is here and I like him too."

By the end of rehearsals, by the final *hallelujah,* I was drenched in sweat. The temperature during the day ranged around 105 degrees with very high humidity. Frank reported that it was one of the hottest seasons on record in the P. I. Aside from choir practice, a general lethargy hung over the camp, just like the stagnant, hot air.

In addition to the heat was the horrible smell from the incinerator. When the wind shifted around from the north, a peculiar sweet, sick odor pervaded the camp. While sitting on the verandah, I saw dark smoke belching from the stacks and wondered aloud what the Japanese were burning.

"It's a crematorium," Frank said. "Dead soldiers are brought in by the truckload and incinerated. Their ashes are then shipped back to their relatives in Japan." Frank saw the look of horror on my face. "Sorry."

Our daily routine was interrupted by one exciting event—a couple inside the camp announced they were getting married. Maggie was an American nurse interned in the camp. Her fiancé was a Filipino doctor she had worked with at the hospital. At the beginning of the war Maggie had lived with her future in-laws, but after the invasion the Japanese rounded her up. Her fiancé and his family were faithful in visiting and eventually persuaded Mr. Yano to allow the ceremony. Once married, the newly-weds would have to continue to live separately.

Men within the camp built a trellis for the couple to stand under for their ceremony. Marty helped sew and fit the wedding dress. Father Jan arranged some lovely music. Everyone pitched in with homespun ingenuity to make sure the wedding went off without a hitch.

"I'm not going to the wedding. Hits a little too close to home, if you know what I mean," Marty lamented. She was cutting down a dress for Mother that Mrs. Urs had brought over. She carefully ripped out the seams, saving the old thread to reuse later.

"Marty, at least you're in love. Look at me. I've never been in love and will probably never marry."

"Pshaw, a lot of good being in love is doing me. I'll be as old as Alice Gundry by the time I get out of here."

I had to laugh.

On the day of the wedding we were all excused from roll call. As promised, the groom's family brought two roasted pigs and many fried chickens for the reception dinner. During the ceremony and afterward, Father Jan played a small fife, and another internee played the accordion while the new couple danced together. Other couples soon joined in. Mother turned and walked slowly back into the school building.

"Hey, I've noticed your Mom." Marty lowered her voice. "Is there something the matter with her, Louise?"

"Oh, she's been like this for a long time. She misses my father."

"Umm, well, care to dance?"

Easter arrived, and the *Messiah* was a success. With Resurrection Sunday came a trickle of hope, news that the Germans and Italians were nearly licked in Africa. The war in the Pacific was beginning to heat up. We all thought, It won't be long now. But as the days stretched on and on, and no news reached the camp, our morale sank to an all-time low. The atmosphere was not improved by the rainy season; spirits were dampened and tempers flared.

The mud and rain kept us indoors. Even the internees' afternoon card games lost their intensity. No one cared about losing or winning.

One grouchy man was constantly hushing Daisy and Mae while they played on the verandah during his siesta time. I learned to tolerate the feel of mud oozing between my toes as I walked to the outhouse and kitchen. Day after day, we ate the same food. Fish-head soup, where the heads floated to the top of the clear broth, magnifying the fish eyes. The same smell of the incinerators, the pushing and shoving by the Japanese guards, the same four walls. All of it was maddening. I wanted to run a thousand miles, jump over the moon, walk the railroad tracks back to Upper Sandusky.

Mrs. Urs came. I sloshed over to the package line to greet her.

"Here is some food and a little something for your trip."

"What trip?" I asked.

"I had a dream that you were going away to another place. So here is some money; don't let the guards see it. It is for you and your mother. I am sorry about your mama, Louise. . . ." Her voice trailed off.

"It's okay, Mrs. Urs."

She jumped back into her previous thought. "Also, money for Freddy. When you see him and your father."

"Don't you need this money for you and Mr. Urs?"

"No, no." Sheepishly, she added, "I sold a silver teapot and a platter for this. It will all come back someday, but for now it is yours."

Mrs. Urs. She was a confusing, capricious, and at times a cranky woman. She was selfish and generous. She had plagued our trip up the mountain. She had saved our lives. I was sad to say good-bye.

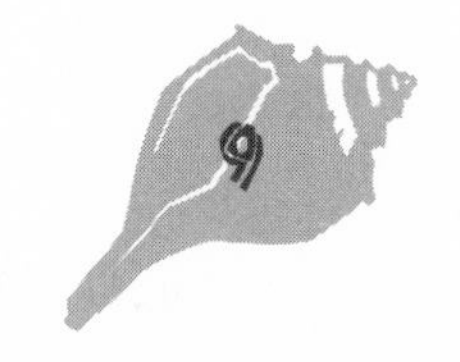

An Invisible Pain

Mrs. Urs was right again. Within a few days the call came. The camp was informed that in two hours we would be leaving.

We waited on the dock to board the MS *Alabat,* while men loaded cargo into the hold and onto the deck—drums of alcohol; bales of smelly, salted carabao hides; and sugar, thousands of sacks of sugar. I was nauseated in the heat, smelling the sweet mixed with the rancidness of the hides. Prisoners of war, young men of the Philamerican army, their shirtsleeves rolled up, some wearing rags, loaded sacks of sugar, forming a human chain. A ballet of motion, a forbidden dance. I turned away, the bright light on the water blinding me.

After all the cargo was loaded, we were ordered onto the boat. By this time we had waited all day in the hot sun. Exhausted, we simply unrolled our mattresses on the open deck and slept under the stars. We picked up more internees in Bacolod, the capital town of Negros Island. Mother's mood seemed to have brightened along the journey. She stood on the deck, peering out onto the sea. At one time, I caught in her expression such a longing that I felt more helpless and scared than I had ever been before.

On the seventh day we reached Manila Bay, passing by an underwater graveyard of sunken American ships and the scarred rocks of Corregidor. The fortress was broken, pitted and dented from bombs and artillery. When my family and I had first come to Manila, we had docked at Pier 7, the longest pier in the world. At that time we were greeted by well-wishers, and there was a festive air about the place. But this time there were no well-wishers to meet the *Alabat*—just Japanese soldiers poised with bayoneted rifles and POWs stripped to their waists, moving cargo around for their guards. I checked the sky: bright sunlight; I wished I were blind.

As we approached the compound of Santo Tomás, I saw tall concrete walls surrounding the former university, a huge area more than my eye could immediately take in. I searched only for one familiar face—Papa's eyes, his smile, his strong shoulders, upon which I could finally rest. "Come on, Mama. We'll see Papa soon." She quickened her pace. I sensed she was excited; her face had lost the look of a machine. At that moment, a real person lived in her body.

A long, circular driveway led to the main building on campus. A wide concrete plaza opened up before us. Internees sat out on the lawn in homemade sling-back chairs, sunning themselves. A man approached us, bowing to our guards.

"I'm part of the welcoming committee. You'll soon learn there are various committees here at STIC. That's short for Santo Tomás Internment Camp." He shook his head. "We get hundreds of new internees in every week."

Mr. Albright stepped forward. "We're here from Iloilo

City on Panay. About one hundred and nine of us."

"Yes, yes, we've been expecting you. Okay, single women to the main building right behind me; women with children to the annex, the small building to the rear of the main building. Men, you go to the gymnasium. Not a lot of privacy; about a thousand of us are stuffed in there."

"It's a shame," said one man in our group, "that more space wasn't provided for the men."

"Well, there was even less space awhile back. We were thinned out on May fourteenth when about eight hundred men left to build a new camp in Los Baños."

The sun poured down on the pavement. A question surfaced in my mind, but I was too weary to give it voice. It had been a long trip, and I was terribly hungry and thirsty. We had been unable to prepare hot meals on the ship because all the cooking gear had been packed away. The only food we had eaten in the last three days was fruit and bread given to us on the dock by Mrs. Urs.

"Arlen Keller, Arlen Keller," Mother mumbled over and over, her words slurred.

"Ma'am, I'm sorry. He isn't here. He and his young friend went to Los Baños about five weeks ago."

Mother collapsed, crumpled onto the hot driveway. I tried to tell them we needed to get out of the sun, eat a little, and revive ourselves, but the welcoming committee wanted to be sure it wasn't a heart attack. Mother went first to the campus hospital, but when she didn't get better and when it was apparent she had other problems, they took her off the grounds to a hospital in the city that dealt with patients such as Mother—people severely disturbed by the war.

So I was alone. I had Alice Gundry and Marty in my dorm, I had the Fletchers spread out over several buildings on the campus, but I felt alone. First I had been separated from Julie, then Papa went away, and now Mother was gone. I shared a room with twenty-six other women of all backgrounds. I lived on the second floor with about four hundred women and shared four toilets and two shower-baths with all of them. There were more than four thousand people interned at STIC, and I was alone.

Once the lights were out and the small nighttime noises of coughing, sniffling, and intermittent cries had diminished, and the security lamps outside my window had blurred, and darkness had filled my head, then I remembered I had a father far away at another camp, living primitively, hacking out a new barracks. I remembered Julie, even farther away. I saw her in the faint moonlight playing hide-and-seek, but before I could reach her, she pulled away and disappeared. And if I stayed awake long enough, I saw my mother's faded face, in pieces on the driveway, like a china doll that had accidentally been dropped and cracked.

One morning, when I thought I would burst from loneliness, a familiar face showed up in the breakfast line—Peter!

Breakfast—one ladle of corn mush
and, if you're good, a little sugar to go on top.
Two lines long, row upon row,
Waiting endlessly for this *and . . .*

Peter of the ship,
Peter of the sea, free,

Peter who looked at me with his sun-bleached hair,
half-cocked smirk, and said,
"How are you doing, kid?"

"Okay." I felt a little embarrassed. I didn't quite remember him being so handsome. I was surprised and flattered that he remembered me. "I'm here with my mom. Actually, she's in the hospital right now and—"

"Is everything all right?"

"She'll be okay once we get to Los Baños; that's where Papa is right now."

"Oh, I see. I nearly got picked to go to Los Baños. A dirty rotten deal."

"Yes, I've heard rumors of the conditions. Men with jungle fevers put to work digging ditches and building barracks. There's little clean water for drinking or bathing."

We sat down outdoors in the plaza in a small square of shade.

"I still have my seashell, the conch I was given in Hawaii. I keep it hidden away—I'm afraid the Japanese might confiscate the one thing that reminds me of the outside world. When I'm alone, I listen to it, waves crashing—it's my link to a place beyond these walls. How are you doing?"

"Okay; well, I'm alive and I'm in here. That's a plus and a negative."

"A perfect balance sheet for a bank clerk."

The half smirk. "Yes. I was in Cebu when the island fell to the Japs. Of course, nothing prepared me for an actual invasion. I never thought the Nips would make it this far. After hearing about Pearl Harbor, we went out to play golf in the afternoon. Cebu has a smashing course."

I imagined a golf course studded with bomb craters. Towns on fire, and Peter obliviously golfing away.

"My father was transferred from here to Los Baños in May. When did you arrive?"

"I came up from Cebu City right before Christmas. It was a dreadful trip. We were a week on a freighter, all stuck below decks. Our baggage was put in a separate hold, so we had no way to change clothes. We weren't allowed up on the top deck to stretch our legs and breathe fresh air. We had to WC out of the portholes—if you get the picture."

"I see," I said, my mush growing cold. "But how is it that you weren't transferred to Los Baños?"

"I heard it might be a rotten place. No water, a lot of hard work. So I faked appendicitis. I got the doc to remove my appendix a day or two before the other men left, and I stayed back to recover."

Peter had a smug look on his face. Top hat and trousers, garden parties, and perks. He could care less if my father had to go to Los Baños. Maybe Papa was never on the list; maybe he and Freddy were numbers 804 and 805. Maybe they shouldn't even have gone, but because Peter had phony appendicitis, they had to go. If Peter hadn't been masquerading around, Papa might have been safe, here to meet Mother and me.

I stood up, standing over Peter, and said, "I haven't seen my father for a year and a half, since he went up to Manila before the war. He was captured there and put here. While you were golfing your way through the war, my papa was a prisoner. My mother and I just missed seeing him. Even now my mother is in the hospital, out of her mind. And . . . and . . . you were afraid." I dumped my mush on Peter's lap. "I have little respect or regard for someone as miserable and frightened as you are." I walked away, trembling in anger.

Peter of the sea, do not remember me.
I am adrift on the waves of sound,
churning and shifting the shore.
I rage, I roar,
remember me no more.

I went to see Mother. Ann got two passes for us to leave the camp for a few hours to visit her at the hospital. Actually, one of the committees secured us the passes. At STIC there was relatively little contact with our guards. The camp was run by committees made up of camp internees. On a large scale the leadership was comprised of many Mr. Albrights and Pastor Smiths—men and women to supervise bathroom detail, an employment committee to decide who worked where, a kitchen committee to buy food for the whole camp, a monitor to say "lights out," take roll call, and report you if you came in past curfew. Marty said there was even a committee to keep track every time someone took a pee. It was just a joke—with an element of truth.

As a teenager I was required to work a four-hour shift. At first I was put on vegetable detail. My group inspected and cleaned the fruit and vegetables bought for or donated to the kitchen. We then peeled the vegetables for a soup. Workers were able to keep their peelings for snacking on later. The vegetable committee was in charge of making sure no one cut their peelings extra thick. If so, there was a committee organized to dole out punishments for those infringing on the rules and policies of the camp.

"It's worse than living in a jail," I told Ann on our bus ride out to the hospital. "At least in a jail, I'd have a cell and a toilet to myself."

"Yes, those toilets can get disgusting. And it's rare when the children get a warm bath. Most of the time the water runs out. Maybe a committee could get us out of this war, huh?" Ann laughed and poked my ribs. "Louise," she continued in a more serious tone, "your mother will not seem like herself."

"I'm not sure what that is anymore."

"What I mean, Louise, is that she might act very peculiar, talk nonsense. You know?"

I crossed my arms and looked out the window. "I want to help her get better. But there seems to be nothing I can do. Mother and I never got along. She's always preferred Julie. Sweet, quiet Julie. Mother doesn't have the patience for my stories, the poetry that pours out of my head. She says I have funny ideas about life."

"I like some of your ideas. They help me to see things differently—sort of like hanging upside down in midair."

I smiled. "Yeah, exactly."

At the hospital, Mother lay like a stone under a white sheet, her face a total blank, her eyes open. She stared out into murky space, a little pool of drool forming around the edge of her mouth. I dabbed it away. Leather shackles held Mother's hands to her sides.

I tried to speak, but the words came out hollow. Sounds of insanity filled the ward: people crying out for a nurse, their mother, other loved ones, perhaps some now dead. A stench filled the crowded room. Patients beside patients, bed after bed, bedpans, a used gauze pad left out in the open—yellow, red, green.

I held my breath. Mother's pain wasn't visible. She didn't call out anyone's name; she didn't bleed or ooze. Her hands and forehead felt cold. I knew her pain—it was inside, and she was just as sick as someone with the measles or mumps. It's terrible when the pain doesn't hurt.

Ann took me out of the ward. "Let's go home."

"Where?" I asked.

"Back to STIC, I mean."

The Pulley

AT STIC MARTY HAD the cot next to mine. It was amazing to see what a human being was able to do with a seven-by-three-foot living space. Under our beds we stowed clothes, charcoal stoves for cooking, eating utensils, and suitcases. Most of the women were honest, but there were a few who wouldn't think twice about stealing a hairbrush or anything else left out in the open.

Chicago Lil was one of the women rumored to be bad. Marty said she had seen Lil's picture in a *True Detective* magazine; she was wanted for the murder of her husband. I heard she kept a kitchen knife under her pillow. Lil was in the habit of staying out past curfew and coming in late, creating a lot of noise in the dark. She bunked across the room from me and at night she snored so loudly that it sounded like a rhinoceros charging.

On par with Lil for obnoxious habits was Hallelujah Hannah. Unbelievably, this was the missionary schoolteacher Papa had been sent to fetch. Hannah was the Baptist Women's League, church choir, and everybody's worst Sunday school teacher all rolled into one. She was a little bit deaf so that she heard only what she wanted to hear; she was blind in one eye so that she saw only what she wanted to see. Hallelujah Hannah dispensed *Hallelujahs* and *Praise Gods* in a loud, ostentatious voice. She had a hymn for almost every occasion. She started every morning by singing, at the top of her lungs, "What a Friend We Have in Jesus."

One afternoon Hannah and Lil got into a fight. Hannah accused Lil of taking a small medicine bottle off of her night table, an overturned vegetable crate.

"You took my special shampoo. I have really fine, brittle hair, and that shampoo helps. With all this sun, a girl has to have her beauty secrets."

"I wasn't bothering any of your so-called beauty secrets. You're off your little Baptist nut, you old biddy," rejoined Lil.

I asked Marty, "What's so special about Hannah's shampoo? It must be a real secret, because I can't find anything beautiful about Hannah."

"Haven't you heard?" Marty said. "She pees in a cup and washes her hair with it. She says it makes her hair soft and shiny."

I had to escape or, at least, get away from all these crazy people. But how could I? There were internees everywhere, living in nipa shacks in the courtyard, sleeping at night in classrooms, packed like sardines in a tin can until there was barely any room left to breathe. I ran out of my dorm, down the stairs, and over to the library.

As I sat down to read Shakespeare's *Hamlet,* Peter approached. I tried to ignore him, but he sat down beside me anyway. He sighed, leaning back in his chair. "Can you believe it? I left London because I was afraid of the bombs. I came here and they found me anyway. I left

England because I didn't want to fight. Here I am—a prisoner of war."

He leaned forward, looking at me, his blue eyes almost liquid. "You're right, Louise. I am afraid. My old man lost everything in the war. A glorious war to end all wars, and here we are slugging it out again, fighting everywhere on the entire damn globe."

Recalling our upper-deck conversation on the way over to the Philippines, I said, "There must be a thousand drums beating in every square, sending parades of men off."

Peter went on, "The soldiers believing it's their destiny to die for their country, their cause. I'm simply not one of them. I can't die for someone else's noble cause."

"I'm not sure what you mean."

"I believe in me first. Whatever affects me the most, I'll fight for it. Right now I'd like to outmaneuver these bastards and show them who is guarding whom. I say let's give the Japs a job to do while they have us in here."

I nodded, trying to follow what he was saying.

He whispered so that I had to lean close to his mouth, "I can get a message to your father."

"How?" I asked. My words echoed in the large room.

"Shush. Just write it down, and I'll make sure he gets it." His eyes scanned the library. We were the only two there besides the older woman behind the checkout desk.

"How can I trust you? This could be a trick."

"Listen, I might be a cad, but I'm on your side. I'm against the Japs just like everyone else in this place."

I bit my lip. "Tell Papa we are all well. Expect us with the next transfer." I went back to reading my book.

Later, once school started, I worked in the camp nursery school. I loved having extra time with Daisy and Mae. Daisy was losing her milk teeth; small gaps interrupted her smile. Her cheeks were no longer rosy and round. Her face had stretched, either from the thin soup or because of her missing teeth.

Daisy thought all the time, always wondering "why." Mae, on the other hand, didn't care about "why." Only if it happened to her was anything ever real. I could talk about the Allied victory at Guadalcanal, and she'd ask me, "When will the rain stop?" I could talk in hushed tones about Fort Santiago, the torture prison the Japanese had set up. Mae was oblivious; it was Daisy who asked her father, "Where did so-and-so go in the black car, and why did they cry so when they came back?"

The Japanese secret police, the *kempetai,* whisked people away in the middle of the night for questioning. Internees caught breaking camp rules, escaping, or hiding radios were sent to Santiago. There the Japanese knew of a painful method of making their prisoners talk—water torture. Prisoners were forced to drink large amounts of water until their stomachs swelled. Guards then jumped on the prisoners, damaging their kidneys.

Classes were one way of interrupting the routine at STIC. The high school students were at all different levels of learning. Some had been at boarding schools in Manila and China, some had been taught the American way, some the British way. Textbooks and materials were scarce. Pieces of chalk and pencil stubs were worn down to nothing. Internee teenagers were in an awkward situation. We weren't actually schoolchildren and we were weren't exactly adults to form a committee and make our own decisions. Instead of going to school many teens opted to work double shifts in exchange for cigarettes, clothes, and more food.

One of my favorite classes was taught by an Anglican priest, Neil Hamilton. He lectured about the metaphysical poets, such as John Donne and George Herbert. One of his first lectures was dedicated to a poem by Herbert titled "The Pulley." I lost patience with this poem. Somehow the pulley was a symbol for something else. There was an abstract idea behind the pulley that I just couldn't get at. I almost quit the class out of frustration.

I complained to Father Hamilton, "There's so much that's beyond my grasp—why do these poets have to make everything so hard to understand? Why can't they write to me and the things I'm experiencing?" I asked.

Father Hamilton smiled. "Maybe Herbert is speaking to you, but you can't hear him right now. Think about it." He tried to explain: "A pulley is a very important piece of equipment for a farmer. It's used in drawing up water from the well, bringing hay up into the loft—a very common device. Herbert wanted to remind all of us that there is something very common in our lives, something we overlook, but perhaps that thing is, in fact, pulling us closer to the one we really love." I felt my stomach muscles tighten, quiver inside of me.

I was so lost. I wanted to be brave for Papa; I wanted to be mature like Marty; I wanted to rescue Mother. How was I to bear so much pressure?

"The pulley," Father Hamilton went on, "provides the tension that will eventually bring us to our goal. What is the pulley in your life?"

I wasn't sure. I did know, though, that the tension would either tear me apart or show me a way out.

• • •

At night Marty sat next to me in the hallway while I wrote poetry and read it to her. She merely nodded and smiled vacantly at me. Marty liked to sit in the half darkness thumbing through old women's magazines.

"Boy, I'd like to make myself a halter top."

I nibbled the end of my pencil. "The Japs won't let you wear it. They just now allowed women to wear shorts."

"Who said anything about wearing it out in the open? I've met a couple fellas who have a nipa shack out in the back campus. They've invited me over for drinks. I might wear it instead of a bra and while lounging slip off my blouse."

"Marty!"

"Hey, Baptist honeysuckle, I'm doing my bit for the guys over here. I didn't earn first place for my sewing skills in the 4-H club for nothing. From a little itty bit of material I can make two halter tops. I'll make one for you too."

"I won't wear it. I've got no boobs."

I leaned back against the wall, distracted by the couple sitting at the far end of the hall. They were completely covered by a blanket. The blanket moved rhythmically, and the gentle, muffled noises disturbed me. There was no place to run, to crash like a wave upon the rocks, to open a sail and glide. Marty continued blabbering. There was no place to hide.

I closed my eyes. I imagined I was walking with Tyler along the railroad tracks. He took my hand and led me under the trestle, where it was cool and dark. We lay next to each other, but I couldn't see his face.

I opened my eyes and found myself alone. Marty had moved down the hallway by the third-floor steps to talk to some men who lived in the small fourth floor classrooms used for high school biology. Overcrowding had forced the camp to find additional space for its men. I recognized Peter among the group. I looked the other way, but too late. He sauntered over.

"Hello, Louise. What are you writing here in the dark?"

I blushed, embarrassed by my previous thoughts. I was thankful for the low lighting, for certainly my face must have been red. "I like to write poetry. It helps me to forget. Forget where I am, this place . . . who I'm talking to," I said, snubbing him.

"Okay, I'll go, but I just wanted to let you know I got that message through to your father."

I started up. "How is he? Is everything okay?"

"Well, I wouldn't be planning a trip to Los Baños too soon. My contacts tell me there's plenty of work to do there. The Japanese want another place like STIC, but the guys have to build eight barracks to hold that many people. In my mind the Japs are getting scared. They see how this war is going and they want to lock up all the enemy aliens as soon as they can. The men are intentionally taking it real slow."

"So everyone's okay there?"

"If you believe me, yeah."

"How do you know?"

"Me and these two Aussie blokes—the other one isn't here right now—we have a setup in the fourth floor laboratory. We've got a receiver and a transmitter hidden up there. The receiver is inside the bald eagle, and the transmitter is inside the toucan." I recalled seeing the ragged, moth-eaten birds in my biology classroom.

"Aren't you afraid of getting caught?" I asked.

Peter laughed at my question. "The commandant would have our heads if he knew it was up there, so mum's the word."

"Loose lips sink ships." I zipped my mouth.

"That's a girl." And he patted my leg. My heart jumped. That night in bed when I dreamed about walking by the railroad tracks, Peter's face was there.

The transfer to Los Baños for the women was delayed, just as Peter had said. I hated telling Mother this news; it might set her back. Every time I visited the hospital I tried to buoy her spirits by mentioning that soon we would all be reunited—Mother, Papa, and me. Mother was slowly coming out of her fog. On recent visits she had been either sitting up in bed or in a small recreation room holding her Bible. Today Ann read to her.

"'We glory in tribulations, knowing that tribulation worketh patience, and patience, experience; and experience, hope: and hope maketh not ashamed; because the love of God is shed abroad in our hearts by the Holy Ghost which is given unto us.' Romans five, verses three through five. Katie, we will not be disappointed if we trust in Him for our strength. Others may fail us, the world may crumble and fall, governments might collapse, but we are safe in His arms."

Mother closed her eyes and nodded. The dayroom was crowded. One woman sat in a corner holding a baby doll. I shuddered and turned away.

"Mom, come back."

Her eyelids fluttered open. "Louise, I do want to come back. It's just so hard." Tears clouded her eyes. "I sit here all day and it seems so dark. I want to climb out. My mother was afraid of the darkness." Mother licked her dry, cracked lips. "She used to sit for hours in her wheelchair at the sanitarium."

I stroked Mother's arm. So thin, so fragile. I wondered if my grandmother had looked like this.

"When I was a little girl, I always believed I killed her. Maybe if I had had more faith . . ." Her voice trailed off. "I wasn't strong like you, Louise."

"I'm not strong, Mother. I'm so confused and I really need you."

"You never needed me. Remember that time you ran away? I looked for you up and down the block. And then before dinner a neighbor came. Knocked on our door with you in her arms. She said she found you wandering down the street. You went searching for a new mother and refused to tell her where you lived. When I reached out for you, you turned away. You would rather have lived with a stranger than claim me as your mother."

"Mama, I do a lot of stupid things, you know. I'm impractical; I spend time doodling instead of setting the table; I stay outside after dark to hear the owls. I'm not like Julie." I felt the tension inside of me. I wanted to rise above this sorrow and take Mother with me. What was it Father Hamilton had said—a pulley drawing me closer to the one I loved. Why can't it be easy, I wondered, instead of so hard?

"It wasn't the tuberculosis that killed your grandmother." I leaned closer to the arm of Mother's chair to hear her soft voice. "She cut her wrists. She committed suicide. She didn't think there was any way out."

I sobbed, "Oh, Mommy."

Ann stroked Mother's neck and back. We all cried

because of the secret Mother had carried inside. A small child remembered what the grown-ups tried to forget.

"Mom, it's okay. It wasn't your fault. Sometimes folks just run out of hope." I groped for the right words. "Hope is like a pulley; it brings us up out of our doom, out of the deep well of darkness. Hope is a powerful thing."

Mother sat for a long time. Shadows lengthened in the room as the sun moved across the afternoon. I rested my head in Mother's lap and let her touch my hair, mussing it, petting me.

I stood up to leave and held out my hand. "Let's go home."

"Where?" she asked.

"Back to STIC."

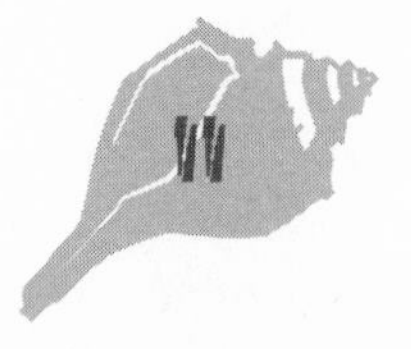

A Far and Distant Drum

Mother moved out of the hospital. She slept in the other bed next to mine and worked in the sewing room. Through the Red Cross we received donations of clothing, some of it unsuitable for the Tropics, most needing to be altered. The sewing committee did everything from making over dresses to mending and repairs. Mother loved the work. "It's what I did at home—only I do it now for about a thousand people." She pressed her lips together, thinking, then said, "It feels good to be needed."

I've heard it said that when a cup is mended it is actually strongest where the glue holds it together. Mother was like that—strong, but still fragile in places. We learned to lean on each other.

Peter brought us news of victories in the Solomon Islands. Little by little, island-hopping, the Allies were coming to get us.

Peter and I were often together, either talking at night on the stairs or coincidentally sitting next to each other at the Theater under the Stars—the internees' name for the camp theatricals. My favorite was "Take It or Leave It," a quiz show where we received prizes such as coconut honey, toothpaste, or similar luxuries for answering bogus questions. At first individuals participated, but later on groups battled it out—for instance, the Hospital Staff vs. the Sanitation and Health Committee or the Canteen vs. the Censors.

One evening Peter stopped beneath a lamp in the plaza and lit a cigarette. The thin smoke disappeared into the yellow light. "Italy has surrendered. That's one down and two to go."

"Gee, that's great. Soon the Allies will be here." The stars in the dark, tropical sky stood out like glittering crystals.

"Afraid not. At least not this year." Already it was November, almost Thanksgiving. Nearly another year of war, and still no surrender in sight.

"I hope you aren't taking too many chances. What if you get caught?"

He leaned back against the wall, letting out a long breath of air and blue smoke. "I'm not afraid of dying. I'd rather die young than whittle away like my father. He lives in a dreamworld, reminiscing about how great the war was, all the while hacking poison out of his lungs and humping around on a fake leg."

"Still, it takes courage to run the risks you do. Why?"

"I take the risk for myself. I'm lazy, really. I don't want to fight, but I don't mind driving the Japs crazy looking for the bloody wireless." He smiled his crooked half smile.

I thought about it and then went ahead and said it: "You are a true coward. You can't even admit you do care about others."

I went upstairs to my area. Mother was getting ready for bed. I was just able to tell her the good war news before lights-out.

About half an hour later there was a ruckus in the hallway. All internees were supposed to be in their beds.

"Quiet out there!" someone yelled. "Go to bed," another voice echoed.

Marty cursed. I heard her bumping into beds, trying to find her own in the darkness. "Go to hell, you old windbags."

Quite by accident, Marty got into bed with Chicago Lil. Soon the lights were on, and I saw Lil and Marty rolling around, struggling with each other up and down the middle aisle.

Hallelujah Hannah started praying. "Lord, I know you despise whores, drunkards, and thieves. Cast down wrath upon these shameful women."

"Oh, shut up," Lil and Marty shouted together. Next they started after Hannah, chasing her around the room. Her squeaky singsong voice found a new pitch.

Soon the guards came to take Lil and Marty away to the camp jail. Marty struggled and cursed. She was drunk. She kept spitting at the guards and repeating, "Saki, saki."

Lights-out once again.

The bell for school rang. I hurried to geology class, which was held in the lab on the fourth floor. Frank Fletcher taught high school geology, biology, and chemistry. There were no textbooks, but Frank lectured from life experience. He was just beginning to discourse on the intense pressure inside the earth's core—the whole disruptive process of seismic seizures, volcanoes, and earthquakes—when a group of Japanese guards burst into the room with rifles pointed, shouting orders in Japanese. Frank backed away from the blackboard. The guards rushed past him to the stuffed birds molting in the corner. With their bayonets, they ripped the birds open. Feathers and dust blew out like a cloud around the guards as they reached their hands inside. From the eagle they pulled out a radio receiver, and out of the toucan came a transmitter. I gasped—how had they known?

Minutes later I heard a scuffle in the plaza. I rushed to the window and saw a black car pull up in the courtyard. Peter and two other men, their hands bound behind their backs, were being led away.

I rushed down the stairs two at a time and came out of the main building just as they were pushing Peter into the car. A choking sound escaped from my throat; Peter looked up. With a half-smirk smile he nodded at me . . . and then the car door closed.

Bang the drum
you pretty girls in the square
Fly your colors high
the garlands you wear in your hair
give a flower to a boy walking by

Bang your drum
in the empty square
the fair-haired lads have all gone
and where they used to be
are petals, crushed and torn

In the ancient, hollow square
beats the strange echo
of marching feet
and drums banging.
Faded, lifeless cheers all 'round

The boys have all gone to war
to fight and die
but on the wind
is heard, far and distant,
the banging of drums
endlessly

I closed my notebook; lights-out. The tense stillness frightened me. Every cough echoed inside my head; the constant rolling and turning and the squeaking of bed-springs were magnified in my ears. In my imagination I saw Peter in a damp, crowded cell at Fort Santiago.

Sometime during the night a storm came up. The wind, always blowing, seemed hardly noticeable, but after about an hour the volume picked up and it turned into a scream, howling in through the cracks in the window. I awoke with a start, thinking it was Peter calling out to me. I didn't want to wake Mother, but the glass in the panes began to shake. I wondered if the fear inside of me had somehow been unleashed into the open night.

"Do you hear it, Louise?"

"Yes, Mother. Are you okay?"

Lamps began to flicker on throughout the room. Mother and I chinked the loose-fitting windows with rags. By morning the wind was driving rain flat across the plaza. It was impossible to distinguish any of the buildings through the gray deluge. Water ran in rivers through our soaked rags; the glass eventually gave way under the pressure. Mother and I moved our beds away from the windows into the middle of the room. I sacrificed my mattress and wedged it up against the window to prevent glass from flying in. We moved our charcoal burner into the hallway and prepared breakfast, a small bowl of rice. The tiny embers provided light to see by in the long, dark morning. By midday the gas and electricity were all off. Notices were posted to boil all drinking water. The plumbing completely backed up. A pail system was improvised to flush the toilets. Emergency lamps that burned coconut oil threw eerie shadows against the walls.

Frank came over in the afternoon to see how we were doing. He literally blew in, bringing a flood of water with him through the open door.

"It's a big one, Kate," he said, smiling. "The barometer dropped the lowest I've ever seen it in the P. I. November usually marks the beginning of the dry season. No chance of that today. Just listen to that wind."

Suddenly an uprooted tree exploded against the side of the building, shattering windows and shaking the walls.

Mother and I screamed.

"My goodness," Mother said. "It sounds like it's trying to get inside."

The monster continued to rage for most of the day, and then about nightfall there was dead calm. We were in the eye of the hurricane. This is how it is, I thought. This is how it is for Peter, waiting in his cell at Santiago. If only he could stay in the shelter of the storm and avoid all harm.

The monster returned with a vengeance. Its black

claws of rain penetrated the doorways. Throughout the night no one slept. We all kept watch over the central stairway. We gauged the water level step by step, hoping the flood wouldn't make it to the second floor.

People were living everywhere, spilling out into the hallways, lining the stairs. Women from the first floor brought their bedding into the second floor rooms. People living in the nipa shacks camped in every available space after their homes floated away. The tight living conditions coupled with the incessant shrieking of the wind pulled at everyone's nerves.

"Damn, my matches won't work." Chicago Lil was trying to light her small burner.

"Here, let me help," offered Mother, leaning over Lil's stove. I hadn't remembered Mother's hair being so gray, or the area under her eyes so dark and shaded. I reached for her hand. She was still pretty.

By the next day the hurricane had passed, and the campus began to dry out. The cleanest, closest blue sky prevailed above the wreckage and rubbish left in the storm's wake. I removed my mattress from our window and gagged from the stinging odor that attacked my nostrils. A bloated, water-logged carcass of a dog had washed up onto the plaza, and isolated pools of brackish water remained on the campus.

I called Mother over to the window. "What is it?" I asked, pointing to a brown object caught in the branches of a tree.

She studied the puzzle for a minute and then answered with a question. "Is it a fish?" Somehow a fish had blown itself out of the ocean and grounded itself in our tree.

"Shall I climb out and get it? I'd love to eat grilled fresh fish." And so we ate fish that night.

After being shut in for a few days, I needed to take a walk and think. Most of the trees had been stripped of leaves, and debris, like papier-mâché, stuck in the tree branches. What was once paradise now looked like a wasteland. I recalled the Sunday-morning hymn we used to sing in Papa's church in Upper: "This is my Father's world, / And to my listening ears, / All nature sings, / And 'round me rings / The music of the spheres." What beauty? It was all gone, washed away, dried up; there was no peace on earth—it had evaporated like the rain after the storm.

I sat down beside a broken chair behind the nursery school annex to read the latest intercamp news bulletin. Suddenly my stomach quivered and my throat tightened as I read the typed sheet:

> THREE MEN, ONE BRITISH, TWO AUSTRALIAN, WERE TORTURED AT SANTIAGO AND FORCED TO DIG THEIR OWN GRAVES. THEY WERE EXECUTED BY A JAPANESE FIRING SQUAD IN FRONT OF THE OPEN GRAVES.

I crushed the newspaper to my breast and squeezed my eyes shut.

Pounding in my ears like a drum was my heartbeat. And in the plaza, scattered among the ruins, were thousands and thousands of petals like medals pinned to monuments. Peter of the Sea, you fooled us all. You were a hero.

12
Christmas at Los Baños

The transfer to Los Baños took place two weeks later. Except for missing Frank, Ann, and the girls, I was glad to leave. Too many memories lingered in the halls and courtyard of STIC. I looked forward to seeing Papa and meeting Freddy Urs. I still had the money for him that his mother had given me before I left Panay.

We traveled by railcar to Los Baños, which was approximately thirty miles south of Manila. Ironically, Los Baños—"the baths"—had been a resort famous for its curative waters. Laguna de Bay, a huge lake, bordered the edge of the town, and nearby was the picturesque volcano Mount Makiling. The internment camp had originally been an agricultural college. It felt odd walking along the rows of fruit trees—tangerine, *kalamansi,* mango, papaya—toward the gate and fences of our prison camp.

We arrived dusty and travel-worn, anxious and excited. I held Mother's hand as we were asked to line up. It was hard to stand at attention for roll call while at the same time my heart was bursting to see Papa. My eyes strained to see the men in the crowd assembling around us. Please, God, let Papa be here.

"Take your bag, miss?" A tall, very thin boy came up beside me.

"Freddy?"

"Yah."

Papa emerged from between the rows of men and took Mother in his arms. My family had never been much for public displays of affection, but today was an exception. Their embrace made up for two years of living apart from each other.

"Your father is a good man," Freddy said, filling in the silence. "We watched out for each other."

After a few minutes Papa came over and gave me a big hug. "Louise. Louise. I barely recognize you."

"Have I changed so much, Papa?"

"Only that you are prettier than I last remember. A grown-up girl whom I hardly know."

I blushed, keeping hold of his arms. All three of us embraced. A million thoughts swam through my head—was this real, were we actually all together at last? I looked from Papa's face to Mother's, and back again. I didn't realize I was crying until tears reached my lips. They tasted sweet.

"Oh, Freddy." I suddenly remembered Freddy. "Here's some money that your mother gave me as we were leaving Panay."

"Keep it. I don't want it."

He was so different from Mrs. Urs. Serious and sensible, with sad black eyes. His dark hair kept falling into his face, and he had to push it away with his hand.

"Freddy was a godsend. I don't know where I would be if he hadn't helped me through a bout of dysentery last winter." Papa drew Freddy into our family circle.

"Maybe we can use the money to buy ourselves a Christmas feast."

On Christmas day the long-awaited Red Cross relief kits finally arrived. Imagine our surprise when we opened the packages and discovered long woolen underwear and flannel nightgowns—obviously meant for prisoners of war in some other location.

Papa laughed, holding up a nightgown. "What do you think, Freddy? Here's a pink one for you and a blue one for me."

The camp kitchen prepared a potluck Christmas meal made up of canned jam, Spam, chocolate bars, and evaporated milk.

After our meal the camp got together for an impromptu game of baseball. Our Japanese guards loved the game but hated losing. Winning was a matter of pride and national honor—for both sides. I cheered from the sidelines, wearing a pink flannel gown. I never laughed so hard in my life to see the men running bases wearing their long underwear. Our team won the game, but the Japanese claimed victory.

Later that night, before curfew, Papa surprised us with presents.

"I traded a man cigarettes for this ring. He said he got it from a Chinaman shortly before Shanghai was evacuated." Papa placed a beautiful ruby ring on Mother's finger. "It was somebody's treasure. I would like to think that an empress wore this ring and that now it belongs to a queen." Mother's eyes teared up. She smiled without speaking.

"And," he said, turning to me, "this queen has a

daughter. A very beautiful daughter. She is the stuff stars and moons are made of. She runs into rivers, climbs trees, and writes the most fantastic poetry ever composed. She writes dreams and wishes and makes them real."

I began to shake my head no. It was my first Christmas in the Philippines with Papa. It was enough to be all together.

"Her father, the king, and her mother, the queen, love her very much." His voice faltered. I wanted to cry, but Freddy was there staring at me. "This is for you, princess—a box to keep all your treasures in." Papa handed me a black lacquer box with gold enameling. A present from the orient, no doubt traded for some precious Red Cross commodity.

I resisted taking it at first. "I used to think living in Upper Sandusky was the most boring thing in the world. Now I can't wait to get back home in time for Christmas next year with Julie. It's funny," I added, wiping my nose on my pink flannel nightgown, "how far away you have to go before you appreciate what you once had."

We sat outside talking on the stoop of Mother and Papa's barracks. At Los Baños, married couples were allowed to live together. Small children stayed with their parents. Freddy lived with the single men, and I lived with the single women in another barracks.

"What was it like two years ago in Manila when the Japanese invaded?" I asked Papa.

"We were forbidden to leave the city. The schoolteacher stayed with a missionary family close by, but Freddy and I stuck together. We thought, First chance we get we'll get on a boat to Panay."

Freddy continued the story. "Air-raid sirens blew day

and night in Manila. On Christmas Eve, instead of colored lights, we saw sparks and flames at the pier. Dockworkers set the petroleum storage tanks on fire. The horizon glowed with these fires. The American soldiers burned warehouses before retreating to Bataan." I pictured in my mind the Manila described by Freddy. A scene out of Revelation.

"We got your cabled message and were able to call home once, but then no more. The telephone wires were cut," Papa said. I remembered that call. "After Hong Kong fell, we knew it was just a matter of time."

"On New Year's Eve we went down to the Pasig River," said Freddy. "Oil running off from the business district was floating on top of the water, on fire. Imagine a river on fire. Soot and ashes filled the sky the next day so that it seemed the sun never came up. When I awoke, I saw the Japanese flag flying from the hotel flagpole. Within a matter of days we were told to report to Rizal Stadium for registration.

"I stayed with Mr. Keller. We helped each other." Freddy's black, piercing eyes accentuated his words.

Papa interrupted the dismal conversation. "We didn't mind leaving STIC—did we, Freddy? I couldn't wait to get away from Hallelujah Hannah." We all laughed.

I leaned against the door frame and looked up at the starry night. It had taken a long time to get here, and I knew I would never forget how good it felt.

My Hut Is in the Spring

DURING THE DRY SEASON, more internees arrived from STIC. Alice Gundry came out and, unfortunately, brought Hallelujah Hannah and Chicago Lil with her. I asked Alice how things were going with the others.

"Reverend Smith has joined a committee. Mr. Albright campaigned for camp bathroom monitor but didn't have enough votes. Mrs. Albright has her hands full with little Rosie. Before I left, Rosie had cut her foot pretty bad while playing in the yard using a piece of metal for a rake. Got the metal embedded in her foot. Mrs. Albright was frantic for a tetanus shot, but there wasn't any. We had to bandage the toddler's foot and hope for the best. Ann and Frank send their love. The girls are growing like weeds."

That season we staged the First Annual Los Baños High School Frolics, a night of humorous skits, music, and a brief medley of Broadway show tunes. It was an unforgettable evening, when internees of all nationalities sat down with Japanese guards to find out what was so funny after all.

The entire high school—a dozen of us—had worked for a month on the program. Nathan Burke and Freddy were seniors; Lucinda Laws and I were juniors, the class of '45. I volunteered to work backstage—changing the few sets, turning the lights on and off during scene changes, and assisting the actors in and out of their costumes. A vigorous display of class spirit and rivalry prevailed as each class competed to outdo the others.

Freddy, usually aloof and stoic, performed a pantomime mimicking an unsuspecting half-asleep internee encountering the camp toilets first thing in the morning. The men who built the camp had designed an ingenious septic system. Water was piped from the tennis courts to a row of outhouses. The toilets consisted of a long flat board with six holes covered by lids. Below the holes was a cement trough lined with a layer of metal. At the high end of the trough was a large water closet, a tank into which water trickled constantly. The tank was balanced in such a way that when the water reached a certain level, the tank tipped forward and emptied into the trough. Complications arose when feces and toilet paper created miniature dams that had to be cleared away manually. We internees had to time things perfectly: If one happened to be using the toilet when a flush occurred, these small dams created an upward surge, making one's bottom wet.

When Freddy's face expressed surprise and then disgust, I laughed so hard I had to sit down. I peeked out from behind the curtain at Mother, thinking she might find the humor in poor taste, but no, she was laughing just as hard.

Rachel Lindo, a sophomore, played Beethoven's "Für Elise" on the piano. Lucinda Laws sang "Home Sweet Home." Many people in the audience had a distracted look on their faces, as if their minds were far away in their homelands.

Nathan came back to get ready for the next act—a skit he had added at the last minute about camp life. I handed him some polka-dot pajamas. "What are these for?" I asked.

"I'm playing Major Iwanaka," he answered with a devilish gleam in his eye.

Major Iwanaka was our somewhat simpleminded commandant. He was an older man who had been drafted by the Japanese to run the camp, but instead spent most of his time puttering around the camp garden in his pajamas. In the afternoons he drank tea in the shade of the officers' barracks, painting snow scenes on white parchment paper.

"Nathan, you'll get in trouble. Please don't." I knew the danger. I had seen Peter taken away. I had seen others taken away, beaten, and brought back with their spirits broken.

"Oh no, don't worry. It'll come off smashing, you'll see." Nathan had been born in Oklahoma, but as a young child he had emigrated with his missionary parents to Japan. Just prior to the war they were forced to leave. Traveling by way of the Philippines, they were caught in Manila after the bombing of Pearl Harbor and never completed their journey home. Nathan didn't remember America at all, only Japan. How ironic to be Japan's prisoner.

I watched from backstage as Nathan, wearing the polka-dot pajamas and extremely oversized phony glasses, pranced around on the stage. Muttering words in Japanese, Nathan pulled out a long, long sheet of toilet paper and began painting stick figures way too large for the paper. Never mind. He decided to keep painting on the wall of the barracks. A guard came up and said, "Sir, the prisoners, they are escaping." Nathan kept on painting, mindless of the guard.

"Sir, there is an air alert." Nathan kept painting over the chest of the guard.

Another guard appeared. "Sir, a typhoon is approaching." Nathan, oblivious, smeared the face and mustache of the guard with paint.

Finally a guard came and said the war was over (everyone in the audience, Japanese guards included, cheered). "Not yet, not yet; I haven't finished my picture!" Our guards rolled in the aisles, holding their stomachs. Even Major Iwanaka, tears rolling down his face, pointed to Nathan and waved his hands.

Nathan was a success. Only he could have pulled it off. He was so charming with his dark-red hair and quick smile flashing. All the high school girls liked him.

The grand finale was a rendition of the title song from the musical *Oklahoma!* The entire cast came out in their Red Cross long underwear and sang.

"Well, that's our show for tonight," Nathan said, "but before everyone goes, I'd like to thank our backstage manager, Louise Keller. Come on out, Louise, and take a bow."

I reluctantly came out and took a bow before the house. Nathan was a sneaky boy, however. "We also want to do one last number, just for Louise." Nathan began to sing "Happy Birthday."

Oh, my gosh. I put my hands up to my red-hot face. I had forgotten entirely that it was my birthday. I was seventeen years old! Time easily slipped away as we waited inside the camps. Time, separated not by minutes but by events—Santo Tomás, Papa gone, Peter, Marty, hurricanes, Christmas, arriving at Los Baños. . . .

I was so happy I forgot to be embarrassed by all the eyes staring at me. Mrs. Downs, another missionary lady, stood up and sang "Happy Birthday" in Chinese. Freddy sang in German, several sang in Tagalog, and some sang in French. Major Iwanaka and our Japanese guards stood clapping and singing "Happy Birthday" to me in Japanese. A mad cacophony of language. There was so much goodwill that I didn't want the evening to end. It was wonderful to be at peace at least for one hour, and to laugh.

The school year was fast coming to a close, but I had one last assignment—an essay explaining the differences between the Japanese and Western people. The differences were obvious—religion, language, ancestral traditions. What about facing the sun in their underwear, slapping women in the face, and the sadistic use of water torture? These people and how they thought were as foreign to me as the man in the moon. I had a week to write the essay; it would be an easy assignment.

In the meantime, I had started a baby-sitting service with my friend Lucinda Laws. There were many small children at Los Baños. The Japanese considered it illegal for couples to have children while interned, but after three years of imprisonment there was no real way to prevent babies from being born. My favorite baby was little Maggie Suchey. Her mother, Elizabeth Suchey, had been a concert violinist with the Manila Symphony. Lucinda and I often watched the Suchey children while Mrs. Suchey and Miss Mary Thinsel practiced together. Elizabeth played the violin while Mary accompanied her on the piano.

Together they rehearsed "Ode to Joy" for a Sunday church service.

One afternoon a guard suddenly walked into their cubicle. His dark, bushy eyebrows and bristling mustache made our bodies flush with fear. I quickly scooped up the baby, who had been banging on a cracker tin with a stick. Mary quit playing and Mrs. Suchey dropped her bow. Many times the guards came into the barracks demanding trinkets or American dollars. The Japanese-issued Mickey Mouse money was almost no good in the Philippines. What did this guard want—a wedding ring, silver from one of our teeth, a candy bar saved from a relief kit?

His intense eyes shifted around the room. Sweat beaded up on his forehead and with his hand he wiped it off. He smiled a wide, menacing grin. "Bombs!" he shouted.

We had all retreated to one end of the room, quivering in a corner. He came closer again, shouting, "Bombs."

I clutched at the baby, expecting at any moment to be catapulted up into the air from a high-impact explosive.

"Pardon?" Mrs. Suchey said.

"Play bombs. I play cello in Formosa before the war. I like bombs. Please"—he pointed to the violin—"please to play bombs."

"Brahms." Elizabeth pronounced the name slowly. "You're asking me to play Brahms?"

He nodded, his face softening into a grin. Squatting in a corner, the guard removed his cap. Elizabeth took up her bow and began to play. As the notes poured out, he closed his eyes—listening not just with his ears but, I thought, with his soul. He moved his arms and hands, his invisible bow across the invisible strings. Together they played a duet.

• • •

One morning I arose early to take a shower. With only twelve showers for the entire camp, the early bird got the birdbath. Often the water dripped rusty and brown through the pipes. It was so hot outside that a person could take a shower and emerge dry, only to get wet from the humidity while dressing.

I usually returned by way of the commandant's barracks. Major Iwanaka was out in the garden before his easel. The pale light of dawn was growing, glittering around the edges of Mount Makiling, the dormant volcano located on the far side of the lake. Major Iwanaka was painting the volcano in watercolors, but instead of a dark mountain he painted it snowcapped and pink. He smiled, pointing to his work.

Mr. Masaki, a new guard, acted as Major Iwanaka's interpreter. "He says this mountain reminds him of his home in Japan. His home is in the mountains of Kiso."

Major Iwanaka dipped his brush in black paint and began a line of Japanese characters along the side of the watercolor drawing. Mr. Masaki said, "Major Iwanaka wants you to know he likes poetry. He has here a poem often attributed to the Buddha, a haiku. Do you know haiku?"

"Yes, I am familiar with haiku. Please tell me what it says."

"It is hard to translate, but I try.

"My hut is in the spring
True, there is nothing in it
There is everything!"

"What does it mean?" I asked.

"It is about death."

I thought for a minute and then said, "Tell Major Iwanaka I write haiku also. This is very good."

My essay at school was due, and I stared at a blank page. I thought back over the past week. The insurmountable differences seemed to melt away. I remembered the Frolics, the baseball games, Major Iwanaka's haiku, and the duet between Mrs. Suchey and the guard. The barriers came tumbling down. After adding up all the differences and all the similarities, I was left with only one conclusion—when the war ended, a new generation must work together to ensure peace.

A Soul Flies Up

THROUGH THE HOT, MUGGY spring, the townspeople came to trade with us. One very pretty young woman, Carmen, pushed a small cart, like a wheelbarrow, down by the front fence. Her prices were reasonable—fifty centavos for duck eggs, thirty-six centavos for chicken eggs—but who could afford to buy? I went to look at the bunches of bananas, papayas, and coconuts. Occasionally she brought coffee beans, which in the heat of the day smelled so rich and good that one would trade anything for just one cup. She offered avocados so ripe, pineapples so sweet, that the air sparkled like sugar. The odor lingered over the hot road. I had a hunger to taste fruit naturally sweet, drink rich cream, sink my mouth into fresh, soft bread. I tantalized myself with these images. I wanted so desperately for life to change, something new to happen.

When the guards were not paying attention, Carmen slipped news to the internees. Freddy and Carmen spoke Tagalog together until the guards, waving their hands and pointing, instructed them to speak English. Quietly she whispered to Freddy, "The Allies are in New Guinea and the Admiralty Islands."

As the days of war stretched on and on, our food rations were also stretched to the limits. One ladle of *lugao,* a rice mixture boiled in an excess of water, was all we received for breakfast. We needed to supplement our meals with food bought from the locals.

When Carmen came, Freddy would often meet her at the gate. One early June afternoon he seemed particularly attentive to her. Afterward I found him behind the gymnasium, out of sight of the Japanese guards. I teased him about Carmen.

"I saw you holding hands with Carmen. You make a great couple—"

"Shush." He put his hand over my mouth. "Listen, I will tell you." He released his hand and pushed an egg toward me.

"What is this?"

"A duck egg. Read it," he whispered.

"What?" I turned the egg over and saw written on it the phrase *D day.* "What does this mean?"

"Carmen told me a few days ago that there has been a build-up of troops off the English coast, that soon an invasion will come."

"An invasion?" I still did not understand.

"Yes, she heard today over the wireless that the Allies have landed in France. In a place called Normandy. Soon they will defeat the Germans and then come for us."

I lunged to hug him.

"Quiet. I don't want the others to suspect that Carmen is bringing us news. She works with the underground, you know."

"Sorry I bugged you about liking her," I said, ashamed.

"It's okay." He walked away smiling a secret smile, a

Mona Lisa kind of smile. I suspected the reason wasn't just D day.

August brought a change in administration. Lieutenant Konishi arrived from Santo Tomás to oversee supplies and food rations. He played more of a direct role in everyday camp life than did Major Iwanaka. Konishi had a mean, pox-scarred face. Ferocious eyes under thick eyebrows and teeth discolored from cigarettes made him look like a dragon. One of the first things he did was cut rations by 20 percent even as new internees arrived daily. He was overheard saying that we would eat grass before he was through with us.

To make matters worse, he banned Carmen and the other townspeople from the camp. He turned them away at the gate, letting the precious food they brought rot on the hot gravel road in 110-degree heat. The sick odor wafted over the fence. To have what I craved within reach only to see it spoil before my eyes was pure torture.

The tide of war was turning, and it was felt within the walls of Los Baños. More people were rounded up and imprisoned. We called the area that housed the nuns and priests the Little Vatican. A low barbwire fence cut through the back campus, separating the Little Vatican from our barracks.

The hungrier we grew, the more tempers flared. One day Chicago Lil and Hallelujah Hannah started their own war. Each woman had the luxury of her own private cubicle because no one else could stand living with either one of them. Lil had taken to earning extra rations by seeing men in her room. One afternoon, as usual, she had a gentleman visitor. I tried to ignore the earthy noises filtering through the thin bamboo walls by reading a *Saturday Evening Post* magazine for the eight hundred millionth time. The words on the page began to fade as the sounds became more and more substantial.

Hallelujah Hannah, not to be outdone, tried to drown out Lil by singing at the top of her voice the old gospel song "Jesus Saves." Within minutes the customer was driven from Lil's bed. He emerged buttoning up his shirt and looking rather sheepish. Lil rushed out behind him, her kimono gaping open in the front, exposing skinny white legs and breasts.

"Christ, what the hell do ya think you're doing?" she screamed at Hannah.

"Pray with me, fall on your knees, hallelujah! Jesus saves," Hannah exclaimed louder yet.

"Oh, quack off!" Lil went into her room and in a minute we heard the Andrews Sisters singing "Boogie Woogie Bugle Boy" at an ear-shattering volume.

Finally I couldn't take any more. "Stop it, stop it. This is so foolish." I went inside Lil's room and ripped the needle off the record.

"Hey, get out," Lil said, "Can't a girl have any privacy around here?"

I looked around her room. Posters lined her walls. One was a recruiting poster: Sleek airmen with white-toothed grins saluted, their wavy black hair in place and perfect. Another poster advertised a cabaret show at a Manila supper club. Dancers, dancers, dancers.

"Lookin' at my posters, huh? I was in this show."

I looked closely at the picture. "Is that you?"

"No, I was just one of the dancers in the chorus line. I never had my name on one of those things."

"I bet it was great dancing on the stage."

"It was okay. A way to earn a living. Not too many choices for a girl to make a buck over here, you know."

"I've never danced." I realized this was the first time we had spoken to each other, even though we had lived together for the past year. "I'm Louise Keller."

"Glad to know you, Louise. I'm Lilly. Never danced. Well, come by some time, and I'll teach ya a few steps."

"Gee, thanks. I'd like that."

At night a blanket of fog rose up over the land, just like a biblical pestilence—a dense fog of mosquitoes. A new chore was added to the list—fire tending. Freddy and Nathan maintained a fire at night around the barracks to ward off the hordes of mosquitoes invading the camp after the first heavy rains. Smoky fires kept the insects at bay.

But like a plague, the mosquitoes struck. Nathan came down with malaria after tending the fires one night. It was an especially virulent form of the disease that attacked the brain. He complained at school one morning of a headache and went home. The next day he was dead.

After hearing the news, I found Freddy on a cement stoop behind the gymnasium. His eyes were red-rimmed. He looked away from me when I came up. There was nothing to say. My own throat was aching from keeping inside the words, the pain of losing Nathan. I sat next to Freddy, waiting for him to speak.

"We got a small fire going and put in some green bamboo to make smoke. Bamboo bombs we called them, because when they heated up they exploded." Freddy wiped his nose on the back of his hand. "We had fun; I'll miss him."

At Nathan's funeral Mrs. Suchey played the violin as he was buried beneath the sandy soil of Los Baños. Major Iwanaka had always liked Nathan; they often spoke together about Japan. Addressing us through his translator, Mr. Masaki, Major Iwanaka described the death of the Buddha.

"There was to the Buddha a beloved disciple named Ananda," translated Mr. Masaki. "As the Buddha lay dying, this disciple came to him with tears in his eyes. He cried out, 'O Lord, who will teach us after you are gone?'

"One of the last lessons of the Buddha was this: Be a lamp unto yourself and from yourself take refuge. Hold fast to the truth as a lamp. And then addressing Ananda, the Buddha said, 'I am on an ancient path. My body is old and worn out. I go willingly to death. Everything created is bound to decay and die. Everything is subject to change. Work out your salvation with diligence.' These were the Buddha's final words." And with this Mr. Iwanaka leaned over and threw into Nathan's grave the rice-paper fragment he had painted months before.

My hut is in the spring
True, there is nothing in it
There is everything!

Oh, how I wanted to fly away and be at rest! I was envious of Nathan. Why did he get to escape Los Baños? Why was I left behind?

Lieutenant Konishi again drastically reduced rations—to three tablespoons of rice per day. Mother experimented with different ways of preparing the rice. She liked to roast it to give it a nutty flavor. I constantly ached inside for food. Not just my stomach, but my whole body yearned for something substantial, something that lay beyond the fences and wire.

Papa joined a new crew that went out foraging for firewood. A small group of men supervised by guards walked the nearby trails around the lake and along the road to town. Papa liked getting out and regularly came back with a mango or orange that had fallen beside the path.

Freddy also joined the wood-gathering crew. One day he returned with a few small duck eggs wrapped up in the tail of his shirt. Papa didn't say anything about it, but I knew ducks didn't lay eggs beside the road.

I had looked forward to my first dance lesson with Lilly, but the very day we planned to begin, I woke up with a fever. By midafternoon my leg had swollen up to my knee with big purple splotches. I wasn't even able to walk to my parents' room for my one meal, so Papa brought it over to me.

Papa took one look at my leg and said, "You must go to the camp hospital, Louise. This is very bad." I was too weak to argue.

Dr. Potter, the chief doctor at Los Baños, examined my leg and said it was a spider bite. "You're having an allergic reaction to the toxin. Normally I would apply a topical antibacterial ointment, but there are no such medicines inside the camp. We'll have to let the poison run its course and watch for possible infection." Simple ailments such as constipation and sore joints were now serious. Our bodies had weakened from malnutrition; an infection was life threatening. Dr. Potter wanted me

to stay in the hospital to keep the wound clean and sterile, and to get extra food rations in me.

Dr. Potter was a feisty man, constantly doing battle with the Japanese. When one of the internees died, Dr. Potter wanted to put starvation as the cause of death on the certificate. Lieutenant Konishi wouldn't let him.

While in the hospital I met Skeetch. His mammoth hands were swollen from beriberi, a vitamin-deficiency disease that affected the joints, causing them to swell. He used to play the honky-tonk piano at clubs in Manila. "These fat fingers ain't gonna play the piano no more," he said with a sigh.

I asked him if he knew Lil.

"Well, I've known a few Lils," he said.

"This one can dance the burley-q."

"I've known a few Lils that danced. Which one you be talking about, young lady?"

"The one who wears a red kimono."

"I think I know the one you mean."

At night the hospital's static walls echoed a myriad of sounds. I heard Skeetch straining to breathe, gasping for air. A mixture of weird noises and awful smells kept me awake. I saw a light on in Dr. Potter's office and limped out to it, using the hallway wall for support. In Dr. Potter's office I discovered a small group of hospital staff and internees listening to an illegal radio.

"Hey, what's going on?"

"Shush, come in quickly," Dr. Potter ordered. I hobbled in and sat down while he pulled a curtain around the area. The radio was stored in a hole dug out of the concrete-block walls. A diagram of the human skeleton usually hung over that space.

"The U.S. forces are in the Philippines," said the announcer from KGEI out of San Francisco. "Some two hundred and twenty-five thousand men swept ashore in Leyte—more men than landed in Normandy. After securing Leyte, the American military will advance toward Manila."

"Can it be that they are here?"

"Not yet," cautioned Dr. Potter. "There's still a lot of ground to cover."

"But surely by Christmas," I argued.

From the radio, using the Voice of Freedom circuit, General MacArthur's voice boomed out, "People of the Philippines, *I* have returned."

A sudden chill came over me.

I couldn't wait to tell Skeetch the good news. "Hold on—they're almost here to get us."

He was breathing slowly, his nostrils flaring in and out. He wet his lips with his tongue. "I can't wait to go home."

When I got out of the hospital, I was still on bedrest. I visited with Lil during the day when she had no other friends over.

"I met a man in the hospital who knew you," I said.

"I wonder who that could be," she said, filing her fingernails. "Damn, my nails keep breaking off and getting shorter."

"His name is Skeetch. He played the piano, maybe at the same places you used to dance at."

"It's possible. I sure do miss dancing." Lilly reminisced. "I worked some of the best dance halls in Manila. One had a patio opening up to Manila Bay. You could dance out one door and in another without your feet stopping. The cool

breezes would come in off the bay, naturally cooling the place off." Lilly floated away, swaying between the columns.

"They played songs by Glenn Miller, Tommy Dorsey, Artie Shaw, and Duke Ellington." I imagined it all: women with their billowing chiffon evening dresses blowing in the breeze, men in fancy suits, the clinking of glasses, the buzz of conversation, and the moonlight.

Lil sat on the edge of her bed, looking down at her feet. "Do you think I'll ever dance again?"

"Sure you will," I answered.

The ash from her cigarette bumped the needle of the record player, causing it to skip.

Skeetch died. Every day more internees died of starvation and disease. A dog, Brownie, a favorite around the camp, suddenly disappeared. It had been a joke with one of the cooks at the hospital, a burly navy man, to reply "Cat and dog stew" whenever anyone asked what was for dinner. One day he didn't look up, but muttered, "Brownie."

News from STIC passed along by new internees was that American squadrons were flying over the camp. I checked the sky daily. Nothing. I was afraid it was just a trick. The tension of waiting wore at me; when would they come?

One day during roll call an announcement went out over the camp loudspeaker: Mail for the internees had arrived. I was breathless—perhaps there would be a letter from Julie. "Keller," boomed the prison guard. I stepped forward and received an envelope postmarked *Upper Sandusky.* My heart raced—it must be from Julie.

Mother's eyes were wet. "You read it, Louise. It has your

name on it." She sat back expectantly. Papa stood holding her hand.

I began to read aloud:

November 5, 1941

Dear Lou,

Hope you got there okay. I sort of forget the island you are going to—is it something called Pancake? Ha-ha. I think it would be great to live on a tropical island. Someday I hope to get out of Upper and go to Columbus. My sister went to Columbus to a secretarial school and learned how to type. She doesn't need to type anymore. She met a wonderful guy and they're going to get married! Wouldn't it be swell to get married?

Speaking of meeting someone, I suppose you heard that your sister Julie is going to the homecoming dance with Walter Krugel. He's a dream.

Remember that dopey kid you used to hang out with—Tyler? He keeps asking me to ask you about sending him a snake. He expected you to send him one through the mail. What a dopey punk!

Well, that's about it. As you know, nothing ever happens here in Upper. My dad is burning leaves in the yard. I love the smell of leaves burning. My uncle has invited me and my brother out to his farm this weekend to help make apple butter. That's great fun—it takes all day for the sauce to cook over an open fire. It sure tastes yummy! Last year it was cold and rainy and I got sick. This year I hope it isn't so miserable. Please write soon.

Your pal,

Sarah Jane Addams

Sarah Jane, my old foe from Upper Sandusky, of all people. Her letter was almost three years old. It had followed me through internment at Iliolo City and Santo Tomás and found me now at Los Baños.

"Well," Mother said, filling in the silence, "the world goes on, spinning on its axis while we are here."

I sat stunned for a minute longer. "Yes, we are still here, starving. I hope they enjoyed their apple butter."

Mother and Papa went back to their barracks. I had to get out of this camp. Climb the fence. Run away. Everything seemed so unfair.

I wanted to escape, to forget for one instant who I was and where I was forced to live. I ran through knee-high grass, the bright sunlight blinding me. I fell down and lay in the tall grass, overcome with emotions. Why, why did Peter and Nathan have to die, why did an acquaintance's letter get through and my sister's never arrive? Why did I have to be brave and strong when I wanted to lie down and die? I wished I was a child again . . . but I couldn't go back—ever. I felt and knew too much already. Exhausted and crazy, weak and empty, I buried my head in the loose dirt and began to cry.

Strangely, angelic voices lifted through the breeze. Looking up, I saw a dark-robed figure blocking out the strong sunlight. I must have run toward the Little Vatican. The nun spoke to me in Spanish, motioning for me to follow her. I took her hand and went into a low building. Strong incense mixed with wax and sulfur rose up in the small room. In another room was a chapel, where the sisters were chanting. We sat down on a wooden bench without speaking.

I didn't know how to talk to a Catholic nun, nor did I

speak much Spanish. "Why, why? *¿Por qué? ¿Por qué?*" I sobbed.

She enclosed me in the flowing fabric of her arms, wiping my dirt- and tear-smudged face with her sleeve. I knew she didn't understand me, so I felt safe spilling out all my secrets.

"Oh, Sister," I said sobbing, "I want a boyfriend so badly that I sit around and dream about being in love. I think about what it must be like to have someone hold me. I feel so desperate and all alone, as if my life will never change. Maybe I'll die and never get a chance to grow up and fall in love, get married, and have babies." I was gasping for breath, I was talking so fast.

"Will I ever find peace?" I tried to think of the Latin word. "Pax . . . ?"

She stroked my hair, cropped short while I was in the hospital with fever. After a while she got up and walked toward the tiers of candles burning against the wall. She lit one and stood praying. The thin light rose up, casting a huge shadow against the wall—a glimmer of hope in the midst of all the chaos. I walked over and lit a candle for Nathan, and others for Skeetch and Peter. I lit a whole row, hoping and wishing and praying for things to change. The singing in the next room had stopped. I heard birds chattering in the jungle beyond the fence.

The nun pressed into my hand a shiny tin star, unrolled from a soup can and finely engraved with a nail. The combination of the late-afternoon sun slanting in through the dusty window and the orange glow of the candles transformed the tin into a bright and shining object in my hands. What a wonderful gift!

"Thanks. *Gracias.*" I gave the sister a hug.

I headed back to my barracks feeling a little lighter. A heavy burden had been lifted. A bird, startled, rose up from the grass. A soul flies up, free at last, I thought.

Crushed, Pressed Down, Waiting

Christmas 1944
Alice Gundry's Recipe
for the Best Potato Pancakes Ever

> Start with leftover mashed potatoes. Add finely chopped onion, salt, and pepper. Knead in flour until no longer sticky. Form a handful of potato mixture into patty and fry in hot bacon fat until golden on both sides. Delicious!

We fed upon our dreams, bittersweet dreams of food and release. Gift giving for our second Christmas in Los Baños revolved around food, our most precious commodity. Alice and I exchanged recipes. Mother had managed to save a can of jam from last year's Red Cross Christmas package. We each got half a teaspoonful. Freddy surprised us with a chicken.

While Mother was preparing our one holiday meal, I took a walk over to see little Maggie Suchey. I had made a doll out of split bamboo for her. As I walked over to the family barracks, I couldn't avoid passing by the corner room belonging to Mr. and Mrs. Leecher. Mr. Leecher ran a black market operation inside the camp. It was rumored that back in the States he had been a con artist and his wife a madam. With this background Leecher was able to make a profit as a prisoner of war. By trading and taking advantage of sick and starving people, he had amassed an empire of emerald rings, wristwatches, and American dollars. In turn he bartered these for more commodities. As I passed by their room, the aroma of hot waffles and real coffee permeated the air.

"I hope they choke on the food and die," I muttered aloud. "It would serve them right, the stingy, greedy thieves."

Beside the barracks I spied the Suchey boys, Jimmy and Robert, digging around looking for salamanders and lizards.

"Hey, Bob, I found one. Mom can fry it up for Christmas dinner. They taste just like bacon!"

I went inside the building with the boys. Mrs. Suchey drifted around the room almost lifeless. The baby was in a corner crying. I picked Maggie up, hoping to quell her screams, but what she wanted I didn't have. The doll managed to hold her attention only for a minute before she began whining and sucking on her fingers.

"Ma'am . . ." I wanted to say something to make it all go away. "Elizabeth—"

"Hush!" Mrs. Suchey cut me off severely. Above the baby's whimpering I heard the sound of machine guns. At first I thought it was our guards—a drill perhaps. The Japanese had been jumpy lately. The Allies were bearing down hard, fighting their way up from the Leyte Gulf.

We ran outside. Other internees were standing and

shading their eyes, looking up to the sky. Up above, banking off a thin, narrow cloud was a Flying Fortress—the Americans were coming! The gunfire was not coming from the ground, but from the sky. A strange, familiar rhythm: *da-da-da dum.*

Elizabeth gasped. "It's Beethoven's Fifth Symphony!"

We had not been forgotten. After three years in captivity, four Christmases after Pearl Harbor, it was like a Christmas card had been dropped from the sky.

Daily, news came to us of Allied victory on the islands of Mindoro and Leyte. American planes reconnoitered above the campus, but we were forbidden to wave to the planes or show emotion to the pilots.

The reins were tightening around us, and as the tension increased, so did our hopes of eventual release. We were surprised when a few days later the ropes snapped and our guards were suddenly gone. In the middle of the night I had heard shouting and trucks shifting gears. The next morning there was no roll call. No jabbering of foreign tongues outside our *sawali* walls. No bowing, no bayonets. Just an eerie silence as the camp was now ours. The Japanese had made a hurried exit.

Los Baños was renamed Camp Freedom. Dr. Potter ran a British and a U.S. flag up the flagpole. On the phonograph we played "The Star-Spangled Banner," sung by Bing Crosby. The Brits sang "God Save the Queen." The storehouses were broken into and the officers' quarters were raided. Gypsy, the camp cook, butchered the commandant's bull and served thick steaks with a double portion of mush for our evening meal.

Our first day of freedom was exhausting. At first we

feared Japanese reprisal, wondered if it was all a sick trick, and then slowly realized . . . we were free. I sat down on the front steps of my barracks, hugging my stomach, enjoying the full feeling. I looked into the jungle and caught a glimpse of Freddy going through the fence.

I jumped up off the stoop and ran after him. "Freddy, are you crazy? You're going to get yourself killed." I caught up with him and grabbed his shirt to pull him back.

He flung my hand away. "Yes, I am crazy." The intensity of his dark eyes scared me.

"Freddy, we're still behind enemy lines. Just because the Japanese aren't inside the compound doesn't mean they aren't out there with their guns pointed right at us."

"It doesn't matter." He started down the path.

"Hey, wait. I might as well go with you," I answered, breathless. "I want to feel what it's like to walk again without being watched. Walk where there are no fences to hold me back."

He smiled. "All right, come along."

I knew where we were going: to Carmen's *bahay-kubo.* I had suspected for a long time that Freddy had been sneaking over the fence to see her, bringing us back eggs, chickens, mung beans, and more.

We soon came upon a barrio, half a dozen houses on stilts clustered together. Carmen greeted us. "*Mabuhay.* Hello." She smiled shyly at Freddy and led us into a large room.

Several family members greeted us, and her mother brought in a tray of fried bananas. Carmen sat next to Freddy and they spoke together in Tagalog. Her clear laugh tinkled like bells. Carmen's mother called out to the other children, and more trays were brought in. Hot *camotes,* a roasted pig, a sweet drink. It was a real-live dream. For months and years our meager food had been the same, and now I was overwhelmed by choices. I floated away in a euphoria of food and of tiny bells, laughing.

Freddy shook me back into reality. "Louise, come. We must go."

I sat up in a haze. Carmen walked with us through the night jungle, back toward the camp. "Soldiers have landed on Luzon. MacArthur and his men are only one hundred miles from Manila," she said in her thick accent.

Soon they will liberate Los Baños. We will all be saved!

We stopped by the fence separating the jungle from the camp. The moon stood out in the black velvet sky. Julie, we are coming home.

"Bahala na," Carmen said. She and Freddy held hands beneath the moonlight and *banja* trees. "I heard a poet once say," she continued, "the past is already a dream, and tomorrow is only a vision; but today, well lived, makes every yesterday a dream of happiness and every tomorrow a vision of hope."

"It is hard for me to forget the past. I'm not sure I can awaken from it so suddenly," replied Freddy, "but I agree that today is what we have. *Bahala na."*

Freddy reached his arms around Carmen and kissed her. I looked away, embarrassed by their passion, yet stirred by their love for each other.

In a minute Freddy called my name, and we went through the fence. Heading back to the barracks, I asked him about *bahala na.* Was it a word for *good-bye*?

"The Filipinos believe everything in the world is preordained, set into its own pattern. *Bahala na* simply means 'let the future take care of itself.'"

"*Bahala na,* Freddy. See you tomorrow." I stayed outdoors for a minute longer, breathing in the cool air.

But the next day the Japanese came back. Again in the middle of the night we heard the rumble of trucks, the scuffing of boots, orders being shouted. Roll call came at six A.M.

Lieutenant Konishi walked up and down the rows, his cigarette breath smothering me. "Anyone leaving the camp will be shot," he warned. I leaned forward and sneaked a glance at Freddy. He wouldn't look at me.

Lieutenant Konishi stopped in front of Dr. Potter, and the two faced off. "And one other thing: I want my shortwave radio back. No questions will be asked."

Silence. No one offered any information.

"Lastly," he continued, "we need male volunteers to dig ditches. Many men needed to dig."

We exchanged glances. Would we be required to dig our own graves?

"Volunteers get extra food ration." A few hands appeared.

Papa was one of the volunteers.

"Oh, Arlen," Mother fretted later, dividing up our rice ration with a tablespoon. "Remember the Geneva Conventions. We don't have to perform these duties; we don't have to sacrifice ourselves."

Papa's face was paper thin. His voice was stern, but trembling. "We don't have to starve to death, Kate." His haggard, weathered skin hung on his cheekbones.

He reached out and tousled my short hair. "You've

always been so strong, Louise. Can you blame me for giving up?"

I barely passed the word *no* through my cracked and blistered lips. In the tropical heat I shivered as Papa stood up and walked away with a shovel. He was a big man, over six feet tall. He probably weighed one hundred and twenty pounds.

Minutes later a shot rang out near the fence by the road. An internee named Pat Hell was killed climbing back into camp from a foraging trip. He had not been there that morning for Lieutenant Konishi's announcement. He lay dead on the road, still clutching a bag of coconuts. His body remained on the hot asphalt all day as a grim reminder to us all. At nightfall the guards gathered his body and buried him without ceremony.

We were dying at the rate of two per day. Papa and the other men barely made a dent with their primitive shovels. We were given unhusked rice and forced to expend precious energy removing the razor-sharp hulls. Failure to make this extra effort resulted in a slow death. Like a thirsty man who drinks salty water, thereby poisoning himself, in desperation some internees ate the unhusked rice and died, bleeding internally, their stomachs and intestines cut and ulcerated.

It was February, a million years ago, that Daisy, Mae, and I had held a Valentine's Day party. Wasn't I Dinah Shore? I couldn't remember; all my memories had hemorrhaged; my bones hurt too much. I went to see Elizabeth and Maggie Suchey. I stopped to pick a hibiscus flower growing near the fence line, thinking it might make a tasty addition to a stew.

Elizabeth reached for the meager gift, her hands cracked and swollen. She sucked in her breath, struggling. "I can't play the violin, Louise."

I held her hands, stroking the palms. Tears ran down my hollow cheeks. Once again I heard shooting. Oh no, I thought, not Freddy. Elizabeth ran to the doorway.

She turned to me, her tired, dark-rimmed eyes brightening. "They're here!"

Men were jumping from airplanes. Their parachutes billowed against the bleached sky. Hundreds of them fell to the ground. Across from the camp, tanks were rumbling down the road. Loud, squeaking metal, straining against a slight rise.

I ran to find Mother. She wasn't in the barracks. I ran quickly to the toilets. I banged on the door and screamed, "Mother, come out." She wasn't at the toilets. Maybe the showers. Soldiers in khaki uniforms were pouring over the grounds, gathering up internees.

"Mother!" I screamed.

"I'm in the shower, Louise. I can't find my wedding ring. It slipped off."

I tore open the door. Mother was still dripping. "Leave it. Come on. The Allies are here. Get dressed."

I hurried to my barracks. I wanted to retrieve my lacquer box before it was too late. I went across the hall to find Lilly. She was standing bewildered in her red kimono. Suddenly an American soldier burst into the room. "You've got five minutes, miss."

Lilly came to life and, seeing Leecher lug two heavy suitcases past her barracks window, turned to the soldier and shouted, "Kill him!" Burdened down by his booty, Leecher's pudgy body waddled beneath the load.

On the way out the door, I met Mother and Alice Gundry, and together we ran across the playing field, where the Japanese and the Americans had played baseball, to the odd-looking tanks waiting for us. "Where's Papa?" I yelled over the roar of the tank motors.

The American soldiers were setting the barracks on fire. Around us was the percussion of machine guns and antiaircraft guns. Suddenly the world was in turmoil, boiling and churning.

Papa appeared in our midst, barely making himself heard above the racket. "You girls get in."

"What about you?" Mother asked, clutching his arm as he handed her into the tank. "No, don't leave me."

"I can't find Freddy. I must go after him."

He disappeared from view as a soldier reached over and closed the door of the tank.

Bahala Na

Mother sat back, wringing her hands. In the tight compartment there were about forty-five women. All of us bedraggled, tired, conscious only of the last fifteen minutes.

Alice finally spoke. "Where are you taking us?"

"Across the lake, ma'am. To Muntinlupa."

"However are we going to get—" Alice was interrupted by a change in the sound of the motor. Sloshing and gurgling. The tank slid into the lake.

"It's an amphibian tractor, ma'am, an amtrac. It can go on land or water."

"Mercy," Alice said, looking all around. "What will they think of next? Submarines that fly?"

I laughed. The American soldier sitting next to me took off his helmet. He looked about as old as Freddy. His dark hair curled along the back of his neck. He glanced over at me.

It was hot in the tank, with little air to circulate. Perspiration poured off my face. I blinked and turned away when the soldier noticed me staring at him.

He nudged me. "Would you like a piece of chocolate?"

My stomach leaped. "No"—I shook my head—"it's been so long, I'm afraid I'll get diarrhea." I cringed at the word *diarrhea.* Why did I have to be so stupid?

Hallelujah Hannah didn't feel any inhibitions. "Well, if she doesn't want it, I'll take it," she said, snatching it out of his hand.

I sighed and turned to Mother. A little white band of skin circled her finger. I knew she was thinking of Papa. I squeezed her hand. "We'll find him again. We didn't come this far only to lose one another."

Mother squeezed my hand back and said, "I'm glad you're here with me, Louise."

I smiled. The soldier nudged me a second time. "Would you like some chewing gum?"

This time I made no mistake; I gladly took a piece. My mouth watered as I unwrapped the shiny foil. The rich spearmint scent overwhelmed my senses. I couldn't remember tasting anything so delicious. I must have looked very satisfied.

"What's your name?" he asked.

"Louise Keller."

"Hi, Louise. My name is Tony Cantelli. Where are you from?"

"A very small place. I'm sure you've never heard of it—Upper Sandusky, Ohio."

"Upper Sandusky—sure I've heard of it. I'm from Cleveland. I used to drive a truck from Cleveland to Columbus. I drove right through Upper. The widest streets I've ever seen."

"That's right. That's how I remember it too."

"Ever been to Cleveland?" he asked.

"No, nowhere except Upper and the Philippines. I've spent the last three years in internment camps, but no, never Cleveland."

"Wow." He shook his head. "Hard to believe all of you were at that place. You've been fighting the war a lot longer than I have."

Hallelujah Hannah interrupted. "Who wants to sing a rousing chorus of 'Jesus Saves'?"

Almost an hour later we arrived at Mamatid Beach. We had to be careful; we were still behind enemy lines. From caves in the cliffs above, Japanese soldiers fired at us. The American soldiers returned the fire, and after a while the shooting stopped.

We finally got out of the amtrac and were able to stretch our legs. Mother searched the beach for signs of Papa and Freddy. Laguna de Bay was nearby, stretched out like a sheet of blue. I had been so close to it yet so far away in Los Baños that I felt I needed to be in it, to know if it was real. I bravely waded out into the water.

"Hey," Tony yelled, "aren't you afraid of being hit?" He tromped out in his boots, his long fatigues growing dark from the water.

I waved my arms high above my head; the wind moved through my shorts and blouse, cooling my body. My fingertips reached; I could almost touch the sky. With my head tipped back, I wanted to drink in the sky, eat the sand and waves—not because I was hungry, but because I was finally free.

I looked at Tony. "How does it feel to be old and young? To go far away from home and then come back? How does it taste to be set free? I want to run, I want to walk, I want to splash." I kicked up my foot with a splash, soaking his leg.

He backed up and squatted on the beach, looking up at me. He shook his head in amazement.

Another group of amtracs pulled up on the shore, and Freddy and Papa got out of one. Mother ran to hug Papa. I smiled at Freddy. I was so happy to see him, but Freddy didn't speak; he only stared distantly down the shore.

Papa whispered, "I caught him going over the wire fence. It was our only chance to escape." Papa shook his head. "He didn't want to come."

Farther down shore, makeshift quarters were arranged for us at Muntinlupa, in the New Bilibid Prison.

"Can you imagine—we left a camp only to be set free in a prison." Alice saw the irony immediately.

"Yeech, this place really stinks," I said.

"And looky here." Alice had turned over her mattress; tiny bedbugs crawled on the underside.

"There must be nests of them living inside these mattresses," Mother said. We dragged the mattresses out into the yard, preferring to sleep on the hard boards of the bunks instead.

Clothing and personal toiletries were provided for us, and food—plenty of it. The soldiers shared generously from their rations. Tony gave me a can of Spam.

"He's taken a fancy to you, he has," said Alice Gundry.

"Oh, Alice, don't be ridiculous. Just because a boy gives me a can of Spam doesn't mean he's in love. Besides, look at me. I'm a worn-out bag of bones. These boys must be desperate, to take a second look at me."

"Nevertheless, watch your heart. Remember what the wise man says in A. E. Housman's poem:

"'Give crowns and pounds and guineas
But not your heart away;
Give pearls away and rubies
But keep your fancy free.'
But I was one-and-twenty,
No use to talk to me.

When I was one-and-twenty
I heard him say again,
'The heart out of the bosom
Was never given in vain;
'Tis paid with sighs a plenty
And sold for endless rue.'
And I am two-and-twenty,
And oh, 'tis true, 'tis true."

I smiled. Oh, 'tis true, 'tis true.

Papa was able to get a cable off to Julie. Some life was coming back into his eyes, but he still found it hard to concentrate. He chewed the end of his pencil. "Louise, you've always been the writer. What should I say?"

I paused a minute. There was a lot to tell. How does one reduce four years into one sentence? "Tell her 'All is well.'" And that is what Papa wrote.

It seemed that Tony was always around, checking to see if we had everything we needed, bringing by more Spam. After a few days Tony was told he was moving up to Manila. I was looking through my lacquer box when he stopped by.

"I saw you with that in the amtrac. What do you have in that box that's so important?"

"Memories."

"Huh?"

I went outdoors and sat down on a wooden crate. Tony sat beside me.

"This," I told him, "is like the Ark of the Covenant that the children of Israel hauled around in the wilderness for forty years."

"I don't get it."

"You know, like in the Bible. The items in this box are important to me—mementos of freedom, gifts from friends—all reminders that my life is much more than war, fences, and fear. This is a conch shell. I got it in Hawaii on our way out. Listen; you can hear the ocean."

He held it up to his ear. His blue eyes shone. "Yeah, I think I hear something, but what's the big deal?"

"I used to listen to this shell before going to bed at night in the internment camps. It reminded me that out there, beyond the fences, the guards, the machine guns, was freedom. I couldn't get enough of hearing the waves wash the beach. I loved the sound of unbroken movement."

Tony nodded. He seemed somewhat baffled by me.

"And this is a photograph of a little Japanese schoolgirl I took while in Yokohama. We made a quick stop there before going on to Hong Kong. I kept this picture to remind me that the Japanese soldiers guarding me were once innocent children. If I could remember that, then I didn't hate them so much."

"I don't think about that when I'm out there fighting. I don't like to think I'm killing someone's father or boyfriend. If I start thinking like that, then I want to quit. Can't quit, though." His hair was greased back off his forehead. A strand had gotten loose and was hanging over one eye. He sure looked handsome.

"And this," I said, holding up my tin star, "was a Christmas present from a nun I met at Los Baños. It reminds me that Christ came into the world to bring peace. At Los Baños it wasn't enough to be brave or good. I needed to know inside of me that real peace existed."

"You sure are cute—a little funny, but cute."

I was surprised and scared. "Funny ha-ha or funny odd?"

He smiled. "No, I take that back. You're the most wonderful girl I've ever met."

Someone thought I was wonderful? I quickly stood up to go. "Thanks. Thanks a lot."

He stood up beside me. I was afraid something was going to happen. I put my hand up to his chest and kept it there. "I think I should go." I felt the blood pumping through the veins of my hand. "Good luck."

New Bilibid was near the front lines less than fifteen miles southeast of Manila. Wisps of tracers punctuated the night sky; sparks fell like stars through the treetops.

I sat out one evening just after arrival with Freddy. Light low on the horizon flickered faintly and then flared. The Americans were holding Manila, but only by a thread. Street fighting block by block characterized the intense battle taking place there.

"I want to go back for her."

"Who? Carmen?"

"Yes. I've made up my mind. I am going to stay in the Philippines. I was born in Switzerland, but I have no memories of it. I was brought here as a young boy. This is my home."

"Home is important," I agreed. "I used to think when I was growing up that I wanted to leave Upper and explore the world. Well, in a couple of weeks I'll turn eighteen, and I can't wait to get back."

"Home is being with the people we love."

"And you love her?"

"Yes. I am leaving tomorrow with a cleanup crew heading that way. They've offered to give me a ride. I want to get her."

A sniper's shot rang out close by. We retreated inside the prison.

I said good-bye to Freddy the next day. I didn't know when I would see him again. The place seemed strangely vacant without him. I was on my bunk reading a paperback left behind by a soldier when suddenly Tony poked his head into my jail cell and said, "Hi, want to go for a ride?" Sure.

We drove into Manila. I wanted to see STIC and my old friends the Fletchers. The jeep bumped up and down over the torn-up streets. Iron sewer grates were missing; broken ends of bridges slanted uselessly into the Pasig River; fragments of walls leaned at impossible angles. It was a tangled mess of steel and brick.

My hair blew over my face and I pulled it away. "I remember the first time I saw Manila. I thought it was the most beautiful city, white like a flower. Now it's like a scene out of Revelation—scorched earth, white smoke rising out of pale ashes."

Tony nodded, looking straight ahead.

As we drove through the gates of STIC, I immediately noticed bomb damage: craters on the lawn, dents on the corners of the main building. The former university had sustained many hits.

I found the Fletchers settled in a nipa shack in the courtyard. Daisy saw me first and came running. She was a big girl, nine years old. Golden curls framed her tan face. Mae was still a little angel.

"Louise, Louise, you've come back." The girls each gave me a big hug.

"Oh, you knew I would."

Ann came out of the shack, so thin and frail I hardly recognized her. A smile wore through. Yes, it was her. We held each other for five minutes without saying a word. Finally Ann asked, "How's your mother?"

I wiped a few tears away with the back of my hand. "She's fine. We talk about you often."

"You'll have to bring her with you next time." And then Ann noticed Tony.

"This is Tony," I said. "He was one of the soldiers that liberated us from Los Baños."

"How do you do? Come inside, y'all. I can offer you a glass of water, but no ice." We laughed. Who in the world ever expected ice?

The Fletchers were looking forward to being repatriated on the next boat out. I talked a bit about Los Baños. Frank wanted to know about the trees and other flora. I told him what little I knew.

"Do you plan to go back and retrieve your insect collection?" I asked him.

"If I can remember where I left it. It's been almost three years. That was a sad day, leaving all my work up there." Frank looked downcast. Ann reached over and touched his arm. "But here's my new collection," he said, pointing to several unexploded bombs, grenades, and other ammunition dislodged from the walls of Santo Tomás.

"Whoa, I'm not sure you want to keep any of that," Tony said, taking a step backward.

"Hey, I disarmed them. They can't go off. I found this baby stuck in the side of the main building over there. Ones like it whistled through the air day and night."

We talked for about an hour. Before Tony and I left, Ann called me over. "It'll be your eighteenth birthday soon. Look, you're a grown woman." She stroked my face and straightened my hair, which had been mussed from the jeep ride. "Take care, Louise, and remember that you're a very special person. My children will never forget you, and most of all *I* will never forget you. If you are ever in Mississippi, stop by and say hey."

I promised her I would. If all my good wishes could have been put into a bottle and given away, I would have given them all to Ann. I squeezed her hand good-bye.

Daisy and Mae brought out to the jeep a drawing they had made. Rummaging through loot left behind by evacuated internees, they had found paper and charcoal. "Here is a picture of me, and you, and Mommy and Daddy," Daisy said.

"And what is that burning thing in the sky?" Had their psyches become so scarred, the images of war so indelibly impressed on them?

"That's a cloud, silly," Daisy replied. "Haven't you ever noticed that when a big cloud gets in the way of the sun, it gets darkened?" What a relief.

As Tony drove into the prison yard, Alice ran out to the jeep waving a letter.

"Mail call," she said. "Got one from your sis." A letter from Julie!

I was almost too excited to say good-bye to Tony. "I guess I'll see you in Upper after the war."

"Yeah." He smiled. "I'll be sure to stop by." He reached out for my hand and held it for a moment. "Go enjoy your letter. Take care."

He drove off, and I hurriedly ripped open the envelope and began to read.

February 25, 1945

Dearest Louise,

I have often wondered about you, prayed for you. Not a day goes by that I do not ask God to watch over you, Mother, and Papa—to keep you all safe.

Are you still the poet? You could always find beauty in everyday things. Your imagination took you places that none of us could find even with a map. I miss you.

Good news. After I graduated from high school, I joined the WACs (Women's Army Corps). I applied and went up to Washington, D.C., with some other girls from high school. We got a room at a boardinghouse. It was hard to live with three girls in one room, but I managed.

I faltered; the words got harder to read. I took a step back and sat down beside the roadway.

Washington, D.C., was busy. It seemed the town never slept. At night there was always a party to go to or a club with a big band. Glenn Miller actually played here before going overseas.

Anyway, sometimes it was fun just to stay home and make fudge.

The really good news is that I met a terrific guy, Tom Myers. He's an officer in the air force. We got married before he had to go over to Europe. He was involved in some of the bombing raids over Berlin, but thank God he is safe. He's coming home about the same time you are. I hope you two get along. Of course you will, he's wonderful.

Cable me as soon as you know when your ship leaves. I'll be waiting for you at the dock.

Love to you, Shakespeare.
Julie

P.S. I remembered I wanted to tell you how my first dance went. It seems so long ago, but it was the last thing we talked about, and you made me promise to tell you everything. It sure was swell. I went with Walter Krugel and another couple. That was the beginning of my dancing career—in fact, I met Tom while dancing. See you soon. Sis

I finished reading the letter and folded it in half and then folded it in half again. I kept going until Julie's letter was the size of a postage stamp. Something inside of me wanted to keep bending it, dividing and creasing the words.

Julie danced at her senior prom. I came down from a mountain to live in an internment camp. I saw a woman get slapped in the face and step back into line. Julie made fudge. I was mother to a mother who didn't know night from day. Julie fell in love while I wasted away, passions and desires subdued before my Japanese guards. I lived my entire teenage years trapped inside a crucible while Julie got on with her life.

I tore the letter into a thousand tiny pieces, my hands shaking. I refused to cry. In the pit of my stomach I felt a burning. I wanted to strike out at the next person I saw.

I walked into the prison yard and stopped short. Freddy was back, sitting on the front steps of my unit. His head was in his hands, his knees drawn up. I stood before him a moment, blocking the sun. He looked up, his eyes wet with tears. He took my hand, pulling me down beside him.

"She's dead, Louise." He burrowed his head into my shoulder.

I was stunned. "Carmen?"

"Yes." He paused and then went on. "I rode with the soldiers back to her village. It was a morning just like those mornings I used to sneak out and see her, before dawn, when the ground was wet. I imagined once again walking in while she was sleeping, her pretty face wrapped in her black hair." He choked.

"What?" I asked.

He swallowed and spoke slowly. "The ground was blackened. The air smelled scorched."

I pulled away in horror. "No, Freddy. No."

He nodded. "The Japanese thought maybe the villagers had betrayed them, had brought the Americans. Out of revenge they drove the families from their houses and tied them to the stilts. They set the houses on fire. We learned this later. Charred bodies scattered over the fields."

He covered his mouth with his hand, crying. I held him for a long while. Tears ran down my cheeks; snot poured out of my nose. I was so tired of hoping. But yet, what was left if we didn't have hope?

"I heard a brave girl once say," I began, "that the past is already a dream, and tomorrow is only a vision; but today, well lived, makes every yesterday a dream of happiness and every tomorrow a vision of hope."

Freddy looked up at me through his tears. "What?"

"*Bahala na,* Freddy; remember?" I wiped my nose on my shirtsleeve. "I don't think Carmen would want us to stay bitter or to seek revenge against the enemy. I've got to believe something good can come out of all this." I shook my head and rubbed my eyes. "Like a pulley, hope tugs at me. I can't waste time hating the Japanese. I can't hate my sister just because fate took me one way and her another." I stopped talking; I didn't know what else to say.

We sat in silence with our arms around each other. *Bahala na.*

17

Ship Ride to Paradise

OUR SHIP LEFT MANILA on Palm Sunday, April 9, 1945—three days after my eighteenth birthday. Freddy came to see Papa, Mother, and me off.

"Well, I guess this is good-bye." He shook Papa's hand.

Papa hugged him. "Son" was all he said.

"Ma'am," he said, hugging Mother. "Thank you."

Lastly, me. This was finally good-bye. He would be taking a steamer over to Panay to meet his parents. I knew no mere handshake or hug could ease my pain of letting go. I closed my eyes to Freddy. While my eyes were closed, I felt a warmth pressing on my mouth. Soft, and then it was over. I opened my eyes in surprise. "I will never forget you, Louise."

My first kiss. If anyone should ask me what a kiss is like, I would say it is like a secret. You can never tell.

The ocean closed in around us. I stayed up top as long as I could to look out over the deck. I wanted to see the sun set over Manila. Soft, shimmering waves of light slipped from the horizon.

Papa came out and stood beside me at the railing. I shivered.

"Are you cold, honey?" he asked.

"No, not really. Papa?"

"Uhm." The sky was gold, streaked.

"Will you dance with me?"

I expected him to say, "Baptists don't dance," but he didn't. He took my hands in his and we began to turn. A cool breeze was coming in off the ocean. The Pacific wind with its melancholy song played for us.

Turn, and I saw a young man with a shock of blond hair, his mouth a half smirk.

Turn, and I was on a mountaintop, the clear, crisp air calling to me.

Turn, and it was summer, a birth and a wedding, and still no Papa.

Turn, and the man with the half smirk disappeared into a car.

I swirled on the promenade deck, hanging on to Papa's neck.

Turn, and there were Papa and Freddy, Elizabeth Suchey and Lil—autumn, and Nathan was dead.

I was eighteen, and this was my first dance.

Turn, and the paratroopers cluttered the sky like small dots: liberation at last.

Turn, and Freddy was saying good-bye.

I was dizzy from the motion. The sky doused, the fire gone out. A slow dance of dreams upon a dreamer descends. The curtain comes down and the music ends.

Acknowledgments

THERE IS NO WAY I could write a book about so many people from all over the world living in the Philippines seventeen years before I was born without the help of a number of resources. First I would like to thank the Chicago Public Library for assisting me in finding out-of-print and obscure firsthand stories of internment during the Japanese occupation of the Philippines. I relied heavily on these resources to build in my mind communities of people living behind fences. Without these firsthand accounts it would have been difficult to imagine the isolation, discouragement, and hope that these people lived with for almost four years. I also want to thank the José Rizal Center here in Chicago and particularly Daniel Catayong for going over my most basic Tagalog. Thanks also to Brooks Williams for his song "Jubilee," which inspired the Christmas story told in the Iloilo camp. Lastly, thank you to Mike and Grace and the JPUSA community in which I live for putting up with a maniac author asking inane questions such as "Is it a radio or a receiver?"

The following is a list of resources I found helpful in my research:

Deliverance at Los Baños. Anthony Arthur. New York: St. Martin's Press, 1985.

Escape to the Hills. James and Ethel Chapman. Lancaster, Pa.: Cattell Press, 1947.

Forgotten Heros: Japan's Imprisonment of American Civilians in the Philippines 1942–1945. An oral history by Michael P. Onorato. Westport, Conn.: Meckler, 1990.

The Japanese Occupation of the Philippines. A. V. H. Hartendorp. Manila: Bookmark, 1967.

The Los Baños Raid: The 11th Airborne Jumps at Dawn. Lt. Gen. E. M. Flanagan, Jr. Novato, Calif.: Presidio Press, 1986.

The Ordeal of Elizabeth Vaughan: A Wartime Diary of the Philippines. Edited by Carol M. Petillo. Athens, Ga.: University of Georgia Press, 1985.

Prisoners of Santo Tomás. Celia Lucas, based on the diaries of Mrs. Isla Corfield. London: Leo Cooper, Ltd., 1975.

The Santo Tomás Story. A. V. H. Hartendorp. New York: McGraw Hill, 1965.

About the Author

JANE HERTENSTEIN is the coauthor, with Marie James, of *Orphan Girl: The Memoir of a Chicago Bag Lady.* An editor at Cornerstone Press Chicago, she lives in the inner city of Chicago. She enjoys doing extreme sports and cross-stitch—but not at the same time.

Ms. Hertenstein will donate a portion of her royalties for this book to help build houses for the residents of Smokey Mountain, a large garbage dump in Manila where hundreds of people live under scraps of metal and cardboard.